The Fixer

Mike Gomes

Published by Mike Gomes, 2017.

This is a work of fiction. Similarities to real people, places, or events are entirely coincidental.

THE FIXER

First edition. September 7, 2017.

Written by Mike Gomes.

For Lynne. Glad you enjoyed it.

Chapter 1

Ice rattled off the side of the glass from the shaking of his hand. No matter how hard he tried, he just could not stop the shaking.

Taking a long pull from the glass of whiskey he hoped to control his fears, but still the shaking wouldn't stop and he knew he could not drink himself blind while he still had a job to do. Calming his hand for just a moment he pulled a pack of cigarettes from his front pocket and patted the side of the box; a habit from years of smoking, though he never really knew why he did it. Struggling to get the cigarette into his mouth he took a deep breath and attempted to regain composure again. Lifting his hand, the cigarette fell from his trembling fingers and hit the floor as if discarded.

"Damn it!" he growled to himself.

Trying to fight was no use. It was going to happen, like it always did, but now was the worst possible time.

"Come on man! Hold it together."

Digging his fingers into the arms of the chair sweat began to drip from his face and run down the back of his neck. The anticipation spiked his anxiety. Thrashing his head from side to side he tried to keep the flashbacks away, but for Michael Falau this had all become a torturingly regular way of life. He could feel the horror coming on and had yet to find a way to combat it.

The large man was built like a doorway, stronger than most and more cunning as well. With dark hair and dark eyes, he bore a scruffy exterior. An unshaven face and second-hand clothes were what most people saw first, just before they'd cross the street to avoid him. But now he sat in a wooden chair fighting the demons in his mind and praying they would leave him alone just this once.

Falau's eyes rolled back into his head as bits and pieces of the flashbacks started shooting through his mind like lightning bolts on a hot summer's night.

The image of a beautiful woman looking at him entered his head. He could see her sitting facing him in the passenger seat of the car. She smiled with a deep love in her eyes. Whispering words he could not hear, he desired to lean closer to her and hear her voice and feel her breath on his neck. Laughing along with her he turned to face her too. No woman had ever looked more beautiful in his eyes. As she shifted herself to lean back against the car door, he pulled to stop at a red light and leaned in to kiss her. Instead she grabbed him around the neck and hugged him, whispering, "I love you," into his ear. As she leaned back again the light turned green and he hit the gas, rolling into the intersection. Glancing back to her with a smile he watched as she tilted her head slightly to the side and gave a coy, playful smile in return.

Without any warning, he saw a pickup truck speeding toward them over her shoulder through the window behind her. Falau's expression changed to horror, as confusion spread over the woman's face. Her eyebrows furrowed at the center above her nose, causing a crinkle in her skin.

The pickup truck made no attempt to stop, crashing into them and impacting the passenger side door. The tortured screeching of twisting metal and shattering glass filled his ears.

Falau jerked in his chair from the impact of his flashback as if he were living through it all over again. Letting out a pained moan he could feel the painful dream letting him go. It had done its job of abusing him. His eyes started to refocus as the last images of blood and pitiful screams filled his head. Gasping hard for air like a man who had just surfaced from too long underwater, his heart raced and he felt like he was going to vomit.

Looking down at his hand he was still clutching the whiskey glass and shaking like an out of rhythm drummer. He lifted the glass hard to his lips, refusing to drink as his hands shook. Tilting his head back the glass crashed against his teeth. He forced the glass to his mouth and drank the remainder of the whiskey in one hit and dropped the glass onto the table next to him as if he had just defeated it in battle.

Clearing his head back into working order he reached over to the table and took a towel and wiped the sweat from his face. He wanted to scream into the towel and expel some of the frustration he felt, but now was no time for self pity. Taking two deep breaths, he regained control of his breathing and finally felt like himself again. He stood from his chair and walked to a wooden door to his right. Leaning into the door he held his ear close, listening for any sound.

He heard a muffled moan. Falau looked down at his watch.

Right on time, he thought.

Picking up a backpack that rested next to the chair, the groans from the next room got louder and the sound of a man's mumbling voice cut through the air.

Picking up his glass again, he refilled it and downed the whiskey.

"Now is the time. All he needs is a little proper motivation. I can get the money and get the hell outta here." Falau downed another whiskey in a single large hit.

"I can do this," Falau whispered to himself.

Chapter 2

Turning and closing the door behind him, Falau entered a room that looked like an average basement in every home. The floor was made of cement and together with the stone walls formed the foundation of the structure. There was only one door to the room and the half windows were boarded up. The space was wide open and free from anything other than a table and a foldout chair.

Walking over to the table he laid his backpack on it and open the flap, but removed nothing. Pushing his hair back from his eyes he turned and sat down, laying his eyes on the man he captured just hours before.

The man on the floor looked at Falau, trying to get his eyes to focus properly. He was young, only in his twenties. His hair was dark and his eyes a deep brown. He was handsome by any person's standards, but not so much that it set him apart from the crowd. He wore jeans and a t-shirt but was missing shoes and a belt. He looked like any other twenty-something trying to shake off a hard night of drinking.

Falau pulled out his pack of cigarettes and banged them against his hand, popping one from the opening. Hands now steady, he drew one from the pack using only his lips. Striking a match, he cupped it in front of the cigarette and lit it.

"Oh, excuse me," Falau said, pulling the cigarette from his mouth and holding in front of him. "You mind if I smoke?"

A look of confusion and anger passed over the face of the man sitting on the floor. He leaned back and looked down at his hands, handcuffed to a thick chain bolted deep into the cement floor. The chain was no more than two-feet long and had links that could not be destroyed by the biggest of bolt cutters.

The man pulled up the chain, frantically trying to yank it from the ground. Grunts and groans flew from his mouth as he put every shred of energy he had into trying to remove the bolt from its deep cement hole.

Rising to his knees he grabbed the chain low and leaned back with all the strength. Once, twice, three times, but still nothing. The chain dropped from his now bleeding hands as his chest heaved up and down from his rapid breathing. Sweat dripped from his nose and chin to the floor as he looked down at the ground.

Falau sat motionless in the chair with his legs crossed and the cigarette still perched between his fingertips as he held it out in front of him.

"All you had to do was say no." Falau smiled, putting out the cigarette on the table.

Breaking his gaze from the cold hard cement of the floor, the man lifted his head and locked eyes with Falau.

"Why?" the man asked, holding his bound hands out in front of him. Confusion filled the man's eyes as he stared at his captor.

"You made this happen. Not me," replied Falau in a matter-of-fact tone.

The man shook his head and looked side to side. He pulled again at the chain but with less force than before.

"I made this happen? Me? How could I make this happen?"

Falau reached for his backpack and turned it to him. Sliding one hand inside he removed a half-filled bottle of water.

"You made it happen because of who you are. The kind of person you are. You have only yourself to blame."

"You're insane. You have the wrong man. I'm just a normal guy," explained the man, turning to Falau, his voice changing from anger, to pleading, and finally begging to be understood. "Are you going to kill me?"

Falau felt a pulse pound hard through his temples. It was the flashbacks again. He strained his eyes to maintain his focus and not regress back into the horror. A female voice echoed inside his mind. *You did this. You killed me.*

Falau quickly stood up, shaking his head. "It's up to you if you live or die."

"What? You mean I can just say I want to go and I can go?" questioned the man.

"I didn't say that. I said it was up to you if you die. You need to be smart and work with me."

"What do you need to know?"

"What's your name?" asked Falau, now sounding more like a detective interrogating a prisoner.

"William Jefferson. But everyone calls me Billy."

"Where did you go to college?"

"Tridon. In the city."

Falau started to pace back and forth in front of the man, occasionally glancing at him out of the corner of his eye. Bring his hand up, he scratched at the scruff that covered his chin after a week without shaving.

"Tridon. They are known for a lot of wild parties. Bet that you have some great stories after four years there."

"Well, yeah. We all had a lot of fun. Why do you want to know about that? It was a long time ago."

"Tridon is an expensive school. You must come from some money."

"Yeah. My parents do okay... Money I can get you. Just let me go, and I'll get as much is you want." Halting his pacing, Falau turned to Billy and crouched down into a low squat. "One of those parties got a little too fun, didn't it? You had a few too many drinks one night and hopped in the nice little BMW mommy and daddy got you and you drove home."

"No! I would never drink and drive!"

"You killed a girl less than a quarter-mile from your parents' house. A girl who lived in your neighborhood all her life."

"No! Noooo!" screamed Billy and he started to yank hard on the chain again. "That wasn't me. I was asleep when that happened..."

Rising up from his crouch Falau methodically walked to the table and reached into the backpack again.

"Please don't kill me! I didn't do a thing. I swear it!" yelled Billy, Falau not even flinching.

Turning around and walking back to Billy, Falau held a plain tan folder in his hand.

"Billy, you're making this very hard on yourself. Look at this picture."

Falau held up a picture of an attractive young female, perhaps in her late teens. Her brown hair fell onto her shoulders and she smiled the smile of someone without a care in the world. She wore a cheerleaders' uniform and had one arm raised into the air. The all-American girl next door.

"This is Erica Snell. But you know that, don't you Billy? She was killed the night you hit her with your car."

"No! No! It wasn't me," Billy cried, shaking his head and starting to wail.

"Billy, look at this other picture. That's your car... look at the damage to the front passenger side. You hit something while going very fast. What was it you told the police you had hit?"

"A dog. And it's true. I did hit a dog! They run all over the place in my neighborhood! Nobody keeps them chained up!"

"That must've been one hell of the big dog. I have hit deer by accident, and my car did not have that much damage. From what I understand the police never came to question you that night. The car was seen by the insurance company the next day, and was in and out of the shop in two days. When I hit the deer I was stuck in a rental for over a week."

"My dad knows the guy who owns the auto body place and told him that I needed the car for school. Please believe me... I would never kill that girl. I even used to babysit her."

Climbing to his feet Falau walked over to the table and tossed the file on it. Pausing to get his thoughts, he felt no oncoming rush from the flashbacks. Taking a sip from the water bottle he turned back around to question Billy again.

"Seems that your father knows a lot of people in town. He's a real estate developer, right?"

"Yeah."

"Lots of money in that field. You can also make other people a lot of money if you tell them the right projects to get in on."

"I guess so."

"Permits, and getting things by inspectors, means a guy needs to know a lot of people at City Hall. Contacts like that would be very useful when his son kills a girl with his car."

"I said I didn't kill her!" screamed Billy, his voice again switching from fear to anger, and again, he yanked on the chain.

Falau was sure if he had broken free he would have attacked him rather than run for the door. He was losing his composure and being broken down bit by bit. Falau smiled.

"It's a fact that he owns the building the repair shop is in. 'Daddy' built the development that most of the cops, including the chief, live in. Did he give them all a break on housing costs due to their public service?"

"My dad is a very well-respected man. He does wonderful things for people!"

"Like letting you get away with murder! You killed Erica with your car! Just admit it!"

"No! I never did that! I hit a dog!" said Billy looking down at the ground, his voice becoming softer and softer. "Some other person hit Erica, not me. I was asleep."

An exasperated sigh left Falau's mouth and he stood up. Shaking his head, he walked over to the backpack and pulled out a folded towel.

"What do you have there? What are you going to do?" asked Billy, flinching at the sound of metal hitting metal.

Without turning or lifting his head, Falau unrolled the towel to reveal several tools.

"Proper motivation."

Spreading the tools out on the towel Falau took inventory of what he had. Pliers, hammer, clamps, nails, and the straight edged razor.

"What the hell is that supposed to mean?" barked Billy.

"It means I'm going to help you find the truth," replied Falau, turning around with the straight edged razor in his hand, opened and in the locked position. The blade was 4-inches long and shone, despite the limited light of the basement.

Terror fell over Billy's face. "No! Come on, man! Whatever you want I can get a for you! Just don't do this!"

Falau walked over, slowly closing the gap between Billy and himself, the razor held firm in his right hand and his eyes locked on Billy's.

"Did you or did you not kill Erica Snell with your car when you were drunk driving?"

"No! I didn't do it. What, do you have cops watching me, trying to bust me for that? I didn't do it! What the hell was she doing out that late anyways?"

As Falau moved closer Billy got to his feet, but the chain kept him from standing up straight. His hands were still down by his thighs and he was unable to raise them any further. He yanked the chain in desperation, trying to rip it from the ground.

Immediately Falau kicked as hard as he could, directly into Billy's stomach. He dropped to his knees and gasped for air. Falau set himself again, and kicked Billy hard in the face, spraying blood from his nose and knocking him to the floor.

Moving with explosive speed Falau stepped on the chain close to Billy's feet, and used his knee to drive him onto his back on the ground.

Falau held the razor within an inch of Billy's eyes. Twisting the blade side-to-side, Billy's eyes locked on the unyielding steel that could do so much damage.

"Do you remember killing Erica Snell now?"

"Yes!" screamed Billy "It was late! Why would she be out there at that time of night! She should've been wearing something bright! I couldn't see her! It wasn't my fault!"

Falau stared down at Billy, now starting to cry. Leaning back Falau rose to his feet and pulled Billy to his knees.

"So, you admit you killed her?"

"Yes. I killed her. I'm sorry. It was an accident."

Slowly turning away, Falau suddenly reached back and grabbed a handful of Billy's hair, pulling himself in close. He ran the razor down Billy's right cheek, leaving a laceration 6-inches long and very deep. For a moment, it looked like a valley between two mountain ranges, but soon the valley filled with blood. Billy screamed out in pain as Falau pushed him to the floor.

"Oh God! Why? Why did you do that? I told you everything!" cried Billy, reaching up and trying to stop the bleeding.

"It's a reminder of what you did. Every time you look in the mirror you will remember," said Falau with cold detachment as he packed up his tools at the table.

The only door in the room opened, revealing a man and a woman in their fifties slowly entering and unable to take their eyes off Billy.

"Mr. and Mrs. Snell?" questioned Billy. "It was an accident! I swear was an accident! I had too much to drink! Everyone drinks and drives! Why was she out there? You should have kept her inside!"

The couple stared back at Billy, not saying a word. A mix of hate, anger and pity etched their faces.

Mr. Snell put out his hand to stop his wife, but he continued making his way to Billy, who lay crying on the floor in a pool of his own blood.

"You killed her. I heard you admit it. After all these years it took this to make you do the right thing. Now you're going to have to pay."

"I said I was sorry. What about forgiveness for me? You're Christian. You have to forgive me, it's in the Bible!" yelled Billy, grasping to anything that might let him taste freedom once more.

"The Bible also says an eye for an eye," said Mrs. Snell in a slow, monotone voice.

Throwing his backpack over his shoulder Falau took two steps towards the door when Mrs. Snell's voice stopped him in his tracks with a request.

"$10,000 to kill him now."

"That's not our agreement," said Falau, turning to look at Mr. Snell.

"I want another agreement. I have an unmarked .38 revolver right here. Pull the trigger, and $10,000 in cash is yours."

"That's not what I do," responded Falau, turning away from the Snells. "That's not who I am."

"Of course that's who you are. Anyone can see it in you. You didn't need to cut him, but you did and you liked doing it. You can't change who you are."

With Mr. Snell's words still hanging in the air, another sharp pain jabbed into the big man's temple. The flashback was soft and distant, but unmistakable, as the voice of a woman saying, "you killed me... it was your fault," rang in his ears once again.

"No!" snapped Falau, taking another step toward the door.

Reaching out and grabbing Falau by the arm, Mr. Snell shouted, "$20,000!" causing Falau to stop again and turn back.

"If you want him dead so bad, you pull the trigger," said Falau, ripping his arm from Mr. Snell's grip. "I'm not a killer!"

Falau walked across the room and through the door, stopping only to grab the bottle of whiskey he'd been drinking earlier, shoving it into his backpack Making his way up the back steps to the door his head started to throb. He knew that flashbacks would be coming again and soon. Turning the handle to the outside door, he heard a single gunshot from the basement. The big man stepped out into the light, happy to leave that place behind.

Chapter 3

Falau made his way down the sidewalk of Massachusetts Avenue in Boston. The sky was filled with clouds that threatened the day with rain at any moment.

Carrying a bag of groceries, he looked at the sky hoping he would just about make it back in time. Making his way up the streets he looked at the old, run-down brownstones and wondered how wonderful the neighborhood was when all the brownstones were occupied by individual families. At one time it housed the Boston elite, but that was a long time ago. Now the buildings were broken up into 6 to 9 apartments, a common bathroom on each floor. Not quite a boardinghouse, just one step above. The buildings were covered in the stains of years of car exhaust and pollution, and the intricate wooden doors were scarred with graffiti. The neighborhood was now the location of Boston's working and non-working poor.

"Mr. Falau is back again!" said an elderly black man sitting on the steps of Falau's building. The man's hair had started to turn gray on the sides and his face was drawn from years of hard times. His clothing was worn down too and lacked any style, but despite it all he still saved a smile for Falau when he saw him.

"Grady! How goes it, old friend?" said Falau, reaching out to shake hands.

Grady was quick to also reach out and use two hands to shake hands with his friend. "I've something you will like," he said with a sly smile.

"Oh, you do?"

"Yes sir," replied Grady, reaching to his side and pulling up a bottle covered in a paper bag. The spout of the bottle poked out of the top of the bag, missing its cap. Grady had obviously been sampling the surprise before Falau got home. "Whiskey. Your favorite. And it ain't none of that cheap stuff. This is top shelf. Well maybe not top shelf, but second from the top. I was thinking maybe you could join me out here and we can make our way through this bottle. You know what they say... if your drink alone you're a drunk ,but if your drink with someone else you're a friend."

"That sounds great. Thanks for thinking of me," replied Falau. "Give me thirty minutes and I'll be back down."

Passing Grady, Falau patted him on the back and took out his keys.

"Oh, Falau, there was a white guy here earlier looking for you. Said you were an old friend but he be dressed like a bill collector. So, I didn't trust him and said you were gone."

"Did he say who he was?"

"Don't know. I asked him, he said he would just catch up with you later. He turned a lot of heads pulling up in that fancy car. You're the only white guy around here so the whole neighborhood is wondering who you done wrong to have a heavy like that sent after you."

"Grady, you know I keep to myself. Probably some jackass serving me with papers for defaulting on a credit card. They can sue me if they want, I have no money to give them. You can't bleed a stone."

"You got that right. You live down here just to keep it real," Grady said laughing at his own joke.

"Yeah. My other house is in Wellesley!"

The two men laughed as Falau opened the door and pushed his way inside, starting up three flights of steps with the bag of groceries pulled in close to his body. The hallway smelled of urine, a smell all too familiar. Falau had learned early on that the mothers would tell their children to urinate in the hallway because it would stop the drug dealers from setting up shop in their building and selling drugs.

Unlocking his door he walked into his studio apartment. He sighed at just how bleak his life had become as he walked across the room and put the bag of groceries on a small table. Across the room sat an old sofa, some patches covered with duct tape and with a sheet pulled over it to hide the holes. A lamp sat on the floor without a shade. Next to the window on the far side of the floor laid a mattress without a box spring. No sheet covered the mattress. Scattered on the floor next to the bed was an ashtray, several discarded cigarettes, and the want ads from the newspaper.

The big man started to unload the groceries when he heard the toilet flush in his bathroom. Freezing up, the big man attempted to assess the situation, carefully listening for footsteps or any noise that might divulge what was happening. Moving next to the table he crouched down, sure that the thief had heard him and had flushed the toilet as a way to let him know he was there. He probably expected whoever was in the main room to flee the apartment as soon as he heard the noise. But Falau had no intention of leaving.

"Mr. Falau. I'm going to come out now. I mean you no harm. I would just like to talk with you. It's been a long time since we've had a talk."

"Come out, but position your hands where I can see them. You do anything I don't like and I'll shoot you."

"Shoot me? You don't have a gun," replied the voice. "You don't recognize my voice?"

The voice rang familiar in Falau's ears, but it had changed. It brought with it a feeling of safety and comfort. The feeling of connection and belonging. All things that have been absent for a long time.

"It's been over ten years. Bet my voice is deeper now. We were just kids back then."

With no effort at all Falau's mind opened with a flood of information at the sight of his old best friend.

"Tyler? Is that you?"

The handle on the bathroom door turned and the door slowly opened, revealing a tall strongman in his late twenties. His hair was cut short and he wore a tailored suit. His hands were in the air as he'd been instructed to do, but he wore a smile on his face that did not show any fear at all.

Walking across the room Falau reached his hand out to his old friend, who reciprocated. The two men hugged and then looked one another over, appraising how their friend had aged over the years.

"Look at you, man. A suit. In shape. Looks like you've been doing well," exclaimed Falau.

"I am. But I have a good place to work and they help take care of me."

Walking to the sofa Falau motioned for his friend to join him.

"I don't have that much time."

"Okay. And how did you find me? Why come here after all this time?" questioned the big man.

"Finding you was easy," said Tyler. "The Internet knows everything. I'm here to offer you a job."

"You remember everything from when you were young?"

"Yeah. I set up a little system to help with that after I got out."

Leaning back on the sofa Tyler's eyes worked their way across the room, taking in all there was to see. "We go way back, so I'm going to be blunt. Look around, man. This sucks! This is no way for you to be living."

"It's not that bad. Jobs have been hard to find, and this is just temporary."

"Five years temporary? That's not just a transition. You're stuck like this. A man with your experience and skills should not be in this situation," Tyler said, with all the sympathy of an angry teacher. "I have a way out of this for you."

"Who said I'm looking for a way out of anything. The people around here good people, and maybe, just maybe, I like it here," snapped Falau. "You show up here after ten years and insult the way I live? The door is right there if this place isn't good enough you."

Raising an eyebrow at the aggression, Tyler leaned toward his old friend. "I meant no offense. Just expecting you to be in a better spot. I know about the part-time job you did recently, and thought you were getting a good income from that."

"What part-time job?"

"Erica Snell."

"How did you know about that?"

"We know everything. I know that Mr. Snell came to you after speaking with a cop who I'm friends with," said Tyler with a sly smile.

"You set that job up for me? Why?"

"Things just worked out. I found you, and figured you could use the money. I knew that you could handle the job."

Pulling himself from the sofa Falau walked across the room, searching his mind for why Tyler would've acted in that manner. Looking to his old friend he asked, "What's the job?"

"Well, it's not exactly legal. But the work is good and it makes you feel good about what you are doing. That's what you're looking for, isn't it?"

"Yeah. What's the job?" asked Falau, more insistent.

"Okay. I'll tell you, but let me make one thing clear: what you're about to hear does not go beyond you and me. If I tell you this, you must keep it to yourself forever. If you say anything about it to anyone at any time, there will be extreme consequences. Do you understand."

"Yes."

"Do you still want to know?"

"Yes."

"The job is simple to explain but hard to accomplish," said Tyler, standing up. Sliding his hands into his pockets he went on. "There are nine judges from around the world. They make up a group that takes a second look at some cases."

"What do you mean, a second look?"

"Nobody knows who the judges are. They only speak to one person. They look at cases where they know justice has not been served for numerous reasons. They need to retry these people, so they need to do that in a more secretive way."

Falau moved over to the window and looked outside, still listening to what Tyler had to say. He could feel the tension starting to build up inside him as he anticipated what Tyler would say next.

"That's where you come in. They like these defendants to be brought in for retrial. As you would guess, they're not willing to do that, so they need to be helped to come back in. Basically, we take the scum that gets let off on technicalities, and give them a trial without all the crap."

"You mean you kill them," said Falau, turning back to look at Tyler.

"Not always. Some have even gone free. The judges just want justice. That's all they care about. This is the purest form of justice you could have. For you it's a chance to be on the right side of good. You can help right the wrongs that the courts screw up so often. You're not a vigilante. You're an agent of change... for the better."

Falau pushed back the hair from his eyes while still looking at the street down below. He couldn't believe that he was speaking with Tyler about this kind of a job. *You should be sitting on the step with Grady and drinking his one-shelf-below-the-top-shelf-whiskey and laughing,* he thought.

"Those days are gone for me. I can't handle that anymore. Too old and too slow."

"You just did it the other day with Billy. I'm not saying it is the same as that snot nosed frat boy. Stakes are higher but it's the same basic idea. You can do it

We need a guy who can work alone or with others. A guy like you understands on the art of cover. A guy like you knows the ins and outs of this work."

Turning back to the room Falau smiled at his longtime friend. "I can't. It's just not for me."

"I can understand that. But I would regret it if I didn't tell you everything. The pay is $25,000 per job. Minimum. And you get to be one of the good guys."

"That's a lot of money. I don't make that much in a year," replied Falau and looking down at the floor. "But I just can't do it. I need to live a normal life. I can't get involved with that kind of mess again. But your secret is safe with me."

"Falau, you can't have a normal life. Not after what we lived through. I'm sure you have a lot of the same problems I do, and the only thing that lets me sleep at night is this work. You need to think about that," explained Tyler. The sharp dressed young man walked across the room and pulled a business card from his pocket. "There's a number on here and I'm the only one who ever picks up the phone. If you change your mind I'm just a call away. I would love to work with you again, old friend. Take care."

"You too."

Falau held the card in his hand as Tyler closed the door behind him. Looking down at the card Falau feared the temptation would prove too strong.

Chapter 4

The window at the far end of the apartment was pulled open. Falau sat on the edge of the window sill looking down at the street wishing he had just stayed on the steps drinking with Grady. From a tall glass filled with whiskey he took a long sip. As day turned into night he could see ambulances rushing up the street, with police cars soon to follow. He could hear the sounds of couples arguing in the apartments around him, often followed by the sound of something smashing due to someone's anger. A drunk stumbled up the street talking to himself. Falau wondered if this was all his future held for him.

Downing the rest of the whiskey he pulled down the window to lock out the outside world. He stumbled into the bathroom, half filled with whiskey and half filled with disappointment at what his life had become. Staring into the mirror he saw a man that was very unhappy. A man that saw no future for himself. Swinging the medicine cabinet open he reached for some of the sleeping pills that had become an all too common feature of his life. They were the one and only thing he could ever count on to help shut out the flashbacks and nightmares that were his tortured past. Well, that, and mixing them with booze. Popping off the top of the bottle he could see there were just a few pills left, maybe just five or six. Dumping them all into his hand he stumbled back out of the bathroom. Slumping down on his bed he the grabbed the half finished bottle of whiskey and threw the pills into his mouth. Taking a long hard slug from the bottle he swilled them down into his stomach. He wasn't sure if that amount of pills was even safe to take, but at this point he didn't care. He took one last hard drag off the bottle, feeling the rush to his head. Placing the bottle on the floor he fell back onto the bed and stared at the ceiling.

"Just one night. Just one night without the dreams. Is that too much to ask?"

Feeling the pills starting to overtake him, his eyes rolled up into the back of his head and he let himself slip into a light sleep.

With the promise of sleep on its way, the sound of an ambulance rushing down the street and its screaming siren broke through his potential slumber. Trying to open his eyes, he couldn't fight the force of the pills now digging deep into his mind, and forcing the sleep to come, despite the distraction of the ambulance.

Deep in the back of his consciousness he slipped into a state caught somewhere between asleep and awake. From there he could hear the scream of a woman and he desperately wanted to help her. The nightmare was coming on strong and there was no way it could be stopped. He felt like he was watching a movie but he was also somehow in the movie. The vision of dark hair zipped across his eyes as he saw the bloodstained mask of a woman's face crossing his field of vision. He thrashed side to side in his bed to try and wake up, but it was no use. He was now stuck in the world where people try to control their dreams and change what's going on. But Falau knew that could never happen. Like every other night before this, it was something he simply needed to endure. It was the worst kind of nightmare, the one where he could think. The ones that he just watched were so much easier. He would just have to go through the torture and come out the other side. In these nightmares, he knew he was simply being tortured, his mind forcing him to see the cold, hard images over and over again.

As he slipped deeper into the dream he found himself in the car again. In the passenger seat was a beautiful woman with dark hair that fell down over her shoulders. She shifted in her seat so her back was against the door and she smiled at him intently with love deep in her eyes. She was everything he'd ever wanted... smart, funny, beautiful, and above all, intelligent. She was the classic girl next door. She would fall in love with him, and he had never felt so lucky.

He approached and stopped at the red light, looking over to her, she smiling at him. Feeling the loving closeness there filled him with undeniable joy.

Without warning he was suddenly in the intersection, looking over the beautiful woman's shoulder through the window at the oncoming truck speeding hard toward them, the logo on the front of the grill getting closer and closer. Flecks of white paint all over the front bumper and dirt that had not been washed off in some time. The metallic green of the hood racing closer and closer. Opening his mouth, nothing but silence came out. He needed to warn her, he needed to let her know, but there was nothing but silence. The truck slammed into the passenger side door, crushing the side of the car and forcing the woman to catapult forward. The smile disappeared from the woman's face as her body lurched and snapped with the powerful impact of the collision.

She flew through the air, crashing her face hard into the steering wheel, her hair wrapped around the wheel, the sudden impact causing her head to stop viciously.

His eyes and head snapped up to the ceiling of the car in an uncontrollable force of power from the crash. He was no longer able to control his head or which direction his body traveled. He lost sight of the beautiful woman for just a moment. Pulling his eyes back down and looking back to her, he could see she had started to recoil and she was falling back off the steering wheel into view. A deep rip cut down the center of her face. The cut ran from her forehead, through her eyebrows, over her nose and down her left cheek, and was filling with blood. Her crushed nose had moved out of position. Her eyes had lost all their sparkle. She stared blankly into the air. She was conscious and she was looking directly at him as if asking him for help. But there was nothing he could do for her. He wanted to reach out for her. He wanted to help her. He wanted to save her from what was about to happen next. But he couldn't. It was beyond his control.

Falau felt his head snapped forward again, causing a great pain to shoot up from his neck and into his back. His hands bounced off the steering wheel, causing the airbag to deploy and force its way into his face. Just as this happened he reached out for the woman, who was incapable of reaching back. Now going hard backwards her head slammed through the broken glass. Her body bent and lifted out through the passenger window, hitting the pickup truck before recoiling again and being forced back into the car. As the airbag started to deflate, he opened his eyes to see her covered with glass. She had fallen into the well of the passenger seat. Her head tilted back as her body had crumbled. Her eyes were open but there was no life. Falau reached out to her, still fighting the airbag, trying to get closer. Shards of glass were embedded deep into her face, causing her to look as if she was wearing a mask. As the airbag deflated he grabbed her hand, shaking it and screaming to her, but there was no response. As he screamed for help he jolted himself out of the drug and alcohol fueled sleep, finally saving him from his nightmare from hell. Breathing hard, his chest sent strong pains shooting down his left arm. His eyes stared at the ceiling and his fists clenched hard as the man took several deep breaths, trying to control his emotions.

"No!" he shouted as his fist turned pounded the mattress. Reaching to the side he grabbed the bottle of whiskey and threw it at the wall, shattering it, and spilling the contents down the wall and him alone with his thoughts. Looking up to the ceiling, tears started to fill his eyes as the big man said, "I'm sorry."

Chapter 5

The sound of the skill saw filled the air and muted the sounds of the hammers crashing down on the nails they were driving home, and the occasional shouts of men moving around the worksite trying to get their jobs done before the end of the day.

"Fuck!" exclaimed Falau, hitting his thumb with a hammer as he started to frame a wall.

"You'd think by now you'd have that down," joked a large man wearing a hard hat. "Who let you have a hammer anyways? I thought you were a laborer."

"I am, but they were short of carpenters so they gave me something easy to do."

"Their mistake. Next thing you know you'll be in line for some injury pay."

Falau laughed with the big man but kept about his work. He was more than happy to be building a wall rather than lugging bricks or shingles, like you would normally do as a laborer. As the day grew longer 3 o'clock hit and all the union members called it a day. There was no such luck for Falau and the other non-union men. They would work until dark and for less pay.

"Hey Falau, get over here," called a short man wearing jeans and a t-shirt, also wearing a hard hat.

"Ya, boss. What's up?"

"You're fired, that's what's up," said the little man without looking up from his clipboard.

"What?" questioned Falau.

"You heard me, you're fired. Nothing can be done about it. We need to cut back," insisted the boss. Dodging the issue with Falau he called to another worker, telling him to get back to work.

"It is something I did wrong? Did I not work hard enough?"

The little man raised his head from his clipboard. "Falau, it's simple. You were the last hired and now you're the first fired. That's the way it goes with construction. It's nothing personal. Just economics."

Falau stood staring into space as his newly ex-boss walked away without so much as saying goodbye. Falau walked over and grabbed his toolbelt and left the final prospect of employment he had.

WALKING UP THE STEPS to his apartment, Falau held a pint of whiskey in his right hand. The bottle was already open and half the contents were inside Falau.

I bet the rich people don't have to climb stairs, he thought, urging his legs to climb one more step and then one more after that.

Turning down the hallway he could see an envelope taped to the door of his apartment. Falau sighed, knowing nobody ever left good news in an envelope taped to the door of your apartment. Snatching it hard from the door he dug his fingers into the seal and opened it. Swaying where he stood, he shook open the paper and started to read:

> Dear Mr. Falau,
>
> We've attempted to reach you no less than two dozen times over the last two months. Each time we have been unable to contact you. We have also been made aware that you have changed the locks on your apartment. This is in clear violation of your tenant agreement.
>
> More alarming than this is the fact that you've not paid rent in over three months. By not returning our attempted contacts to you, and the lack of payment, you leave us no choice but to evict you from your apartment. You have one week in which to remove all your things and move out. If you do not comply, the local sheriff will be contacted to force your removal.
>
> All the best,

Arthur Steinberg

Falau's head shook as he finished the letter. Having no money and no job, he crumpled the letter in his hand and threw it on the ground. Taking another long sip from the bottle, he fished in his pocket for the keys to unlock the door. Unsteady on his feet he bumped into the door frame as his key slipped into the lock and he pushed the door open.

"Home sweet home," he mumbled to himself, taking another sip from the bottle slamming the door closed with a kick.

Staggering across the room Falau dropped himself on the sofa, causing the covering sheet to fall off the back. Resting his head back on the sofa he felt the internal foam against his head. Reaching back, he could feel the exposed internal springs of the sofa pressing against his head.

"I can't even afford a real sofa," complained Falau to nobody but himself, his words slurred. Taking a handful of the foam, he ripped it from the sofa and threw it down on the floor. "Not even a decent sofa. How can a man my age not have decent furniture? I'm such a loser, I can't even afford to get a sofa that doesn't have holes in it!"

Without warning a flash of the bloodied face of the woman he loved falling back across the car after the impact of the crash passed before his eyes, the sound of the voice calling out, "You did it... it's your fault, echoing in his mind.

Shaking his head, he attempted to remove the horror from his mind but it would not let go. The image of the pickup crashing into the passenger side of the car replayed over and over again in his head. One impact after another. The metal and glass breaking. The look crossing the face of the woman as her body absorbed the impact of the crash.

Fighting the flashback Falau downed the rest of the whiskey. Drinking himself into unconsciousness was one of the only things he felt he could do in times like this. The bottle fell to the floor as the whiskey hit him hard. His head dropping back, he caught sight of the exposed pipes running across the ceiling in his apartment.

Slurring his words he mumbled, "...couldn't even give me a decent ceiling. Exposed pipes. A slum..."

The big man's eyes did not leave the pipes. Examining them, he felt they were strong and sturdy, a lot like the ones he helped install on a construction job downtown.

Falau pulled his drunk self-up and walked over to the table at the far end of the room and took the chair that sat behind it. Dragging the chair and shaking it as he went, he tested it for strength.

"Yeah, that'll hold me."

Drunk with a pint of whiskey inside him, he gingerly pulled himself onto the chair in the standing position. The chair quivered and he waited for it to shoot out from under him if he put too much weight to anyone side.

Placing his hands above his head the big man reached up and grabbed the pipe. Slowly placing his weight on it he felt the pipe move downward in the holes cut at either end of the room. Falau lifted his feet off the chair and started to swing. A smile crossed his face as he hung from the pipe. No sooner had the smile came than it disappeared, as he realized the pipe would hold his weight after all.

Dropping his feet back to the chair he regained his balance and looked again up at the pipe. His hands dropped and he unbuckled the belt from his pants. The belt was leather and strong, with slight wear marks. Falau had got it at the Salvation Army and he knew it was in better shape than anything he owned. He pulled the belt in his hands, feeling how strong it was before he reached up and fed it over the pipe. He took the leather, fed it through the buckle, and clasped it.

Grabbing the belt with two hands he pulled down hard on it. "If I jump hard that should do it," he said, in a matter-of-fact tone.

Inching his way closer to the edge of the chair the big man pulled the belt tighter and toward him. Leaning forward he got his head close to the belt and attempted to slide his head through the loop.

"Lord forgive me," he whispered.

Before he could get the belt around his neck his weight shifted the chair and it shot out from under him. Momentarily he felt he was hanging in the air and that the belt would snap his neck, causing all the pain to stop. But his body dropped, and he could see the belt hanging from the pipe as he fell to the ground, crashing off the coffee table and breaking it in half under the weight of his large and powerful body.

Falau felt pain shoot across his back from the impact on the table as he lay on the floor looking back up at the pipe. Raising one hand up into the air as if to grab the belt again, Falau moaned in pain, as much emotional as physical.

"Constant failure," Falau said, reflecting on himself and all that he was not.

Rolling over he got to his hands and knees and started to stand up. Pushing the rubble of the broken coffee table aside he saw the business card Tyler had given him among the broken pieces of the table.

Reaching down to pick it up, he inspected the number. Nodding his head, he started to laugh.

"You got me, Ty."

Chapter 6

The black four-door Mercedes pulled up, screeching to a halt in front of the building. Falau sat on the steps looking over as he saw the passenger window come down.

"Let's go", said Tyler, leaning across the passenger side seat and pushing open the door.

Falau made his way across the sidewalk and hopped into the waiting car. All eyes in the neighborhood were watching to see exactly what their neighbor was up to. Before fully swinging the door shut Tyler screeched away from the sidewalk and was on his way down Massachusetts Avenue. Shifting his eyes to the dash, Falau could see Tyler had the car going 60 miles an hour on a main road on the streets of Boston at 2 o'clock in the afternoon.

"Nice power. What's the rush?" asked Falau.

"No rush at all. Don't worry about it, I have it under control," replied Tyler as he smiled over at his long-time friend.

Tyler proceeded to weave in and out of cars, pulling over at random spots and pulling in and out of parking lots as if it was all a normal thing to do. The constant screeching of tires and jamming of brakes made Falau feel nauseous.

"You caught on yet?" asked Tyler.

"Yeah, I think I've figured it out. You're checking to see if anyone's tailing us."

"You learn fast. It's good to have you on the team," Tyler replied, gripping he wheel tight as the Mercedes dug into another sharp corner. "I love that you alled. Does this mean you're ready to join us on a mission?"

Falau fidgeted in his seat and leaned his head back slightly on the head rest. Yeah, I'm ready," said the big man.

"That's good. I have one for you. It's middle-of-the-road for the kind of work we do, but think it's a good one to get your feet wet on," said Tyler, shifting the car again abruptly to the side.

"Instead of driving like this wouldn't it be easier just to try to blend in with everybody else?" asked Falau with a smirk as he grabbed the dashboard around a tight corner.

Reaching out Tyler shook Falau's hand. "Welcome aboard." Releasing his grip, he leaned forward and opened the glove compartment, pulling out a small envelope. Giving the envelope to Falau he continued to move in and out of the traffic.

"This is just some walking around money. You'll need it for where you going to. It can get pretty expensive there."

Opening the envelope exposed thousands of dollars in different currencies. He quickly slid it into his jacket and out of sight. "That will come in handy," said Falau wondering if what he had said was true.

"Okay, let me make one thing clear to you right now. Nobody knows who we are. Nobody knows what we do. Because of that, everything is far more complicated. This means that you're going to be watched by different people. Just like I am watched by people every single day. The inside word is that they think I'm part of an international drug running cartel, so they have me on constant surveillance, exactly what the judges want. Doesn't matter what country I go to, their Secret Service is always right on me. I let them follow me and I let them see what I'm doing until I don't want them to follow me and don't want them to see what I'm doing. This keeps their eyes on me and not on the judges or the system that we've built. I'm the guy they focus on, the guy that they come after," explained Tyler with all the seriousness he could muster.

"Seems like a lot to take on, more than any one guy should have to."

"It's really not that bad. I'm just giving these guys the slip sometimes and then helping them catch up at other times. They're just doing their jobs, and they never can find anything because I never do anything that they're looking for. They just keep trying to get close to me and figure out what I'm up to."

Holding the wheel hard he ripped into a parking garage, not stopping fo a ticket. He raced down to the end of the aisle, cutting hard to the right to go down another level. Reaching the bottom floor, screeches echoed off the wal as his tires dug hard into each turn, the sound bouncing back off the walls like kids screaming into the Grand Canyon.

"All this just for me?" quipped Falau as they came to a stop in the parking spot with a large garage door in front of it.

Tyler jumped out of the car went over to an access panel and entered a code before waving his friend over. Falau got out of the car, careful not to move too close. He didn't want to give Tyler any reason to think that he was looking at the code. Hearing a loud clicking noise, Tyler walked over, grabbed the bottom of the door, and pulled the garage door up to revealing a large area for his car.

Falau caught up to Tyler inside the garage. Turning around, Tyler pulled the garage door closed and jammed on the lock.

"You leave your car there?"

Tyler laughed turning to his old friend. "The door is not to keep my car in, it is to keep everybody else out. This is not your ordinary garage."

Tyler pushed the tool rack aside to reveal the trapdoor in the floor. Popping the door up he flipped the switch to turn the lights on. Then he went down a ladder about 10-feet to a dirt floor that was small and cramped. Without hesitation Falau worked his way down the ladder. On the dirt floor, the two men had to crouch low to make their way into a tunnel that was no larger than 4-feet tall and 2-feet wide. The reason for the size of the tunnel was obvious to Falau: It would deter anyone who made their way into it. This was the kind of place that someone could easily get stuck, and it would cost them their life not being able to find their way out. As they moved along there were various turns and offshoots that would confuse anybody that had entered the system of catacombs. Tyler wove his way in and out to the amazement of Falau. He knew it all too well and made no hesitation taking turns or doubling back at any time. He had clearly ran this course hundreds of times before.

Reaching a ladder, he turned back to his old friend. "This is it. Only go through the door if you're fully with us. You will see things and learn things that nobody else knows. And for everything that goes along with that, there is a price. This is no summer camp, and you're not allowed to just walk away. I vouched for you. I told them who you were, and they trusted me. I hope that I can trust you."

Falau smiled, showing Tyler had nothing to worry about. "I'm ready to take this on. Who knows, maybe it's a second career..."

Tyler patted the back of his old friend and climbed the ladder. Tyler knocked on the door in a rhythmic pattern that resembled a jazz tune. The door slid open and the two men climbed up and into the room.

Falau didn't dare wipe the dust off his body in the beautiful room, with hardwood floors, a large oak desk, some leather clad furniture, and walls lined with books. He smiled, realizing the room probably cost more than everything he had ever owned in his entire life.

Tyler straightened his jacket and walked over to a bar adorned with decanters filled with numerous spirits. "You want a drink?"

Before Falau could respond a voice boomed out from above. "He doesn't need a drink," said the mysterious voice of a man that had been altered with electronics.

Tyler turned to Falau with a smile and a drink in his hand. "They don't trust you. At least not yet."

A look of frustration settled over Falau and his hands balled up into fists. "There needs to be some kind of trust for us to do this kind of work. I can't just go on any mission you want me to. Trust is a two-way street, and I need to know there's some from you."

Again, the voice from above boomed out. "You want to leave, or do you want to stay?"

Falau stood silent, looking up at the ceiling. Frustrated by being able to speak to anyone, he started to pace the room.

The voice spoke out again. "Mr. Falau, this group and the system will live on, with or without you. We do not need you. It is my understanding that you can help us with our work and that you're willing to do some for us. But please understand you're doing us no favors. We have let you get this far because we think that you're capable of doing good. It's totally up to you whether you choose to go forward with this or not. But I need a commitment one way of the other, right here, right now. You can let your pride get the best of you, or you could do something meaningful with your life. It's totally up to you."

Falau stopped pacing and sat down on the couch, looking directly up at the ceiling. "It's just that I feel stupid talking to the ceiling," he said in a sarcastic tone. "You have to admit it's a little bit silly."

"I can understand your feelings about this, but you must note that all con tact is with Tyler only. This is his mission and that is what he does. It helps u keep the system in order. Too many people knowing too many things leads to too many problems."

Shaking his head in agreement, Falau could fully understand what he was talking about. But he still wanted to know who the man he was going to work for really was. The voice spoke again, this time in a calmer, more relaxed tone. "At the end of each mission you can choose whether you wish to be in or out going forward. All we ask is that you never say anything about what you do. I can tell you that no person who has ever been a member of this team has ever left, and no one has ever opted out."

Walking in front of Falau, Tyler took a sip of his beverage. "You see Falau, the mission here is to bring people back for justice. Just like I told you before. But we would never be able to do this without keeping contact to a minimum. You're going to be one of many guys and women who do this kind of work in different corners of the world."

Falau smiled and crossed his arms in front of his chest. "And maybe kill people."

"Who said anything about that?" said Tyler, his tone now one of anger before the great voice in the ceiling intervened again.

"Sometimes we need to kill someone. It is the ugly part of what we do. Nobody likes it. If we do kill someone it is in the face of overwhelming evidence. Just to put your mind at ease, people that have been hurt by the system are clearly people who have done great damage."

"Justice takes on many forms," agreed Falau.

"Yes, it does," said the voice.

Tyler walked across the room to the desk set against the wall and removed the file from the top drawer. Bringing the file over, he opened it and handed it to the big man. At first glance he could see the face of a hardened man of South American descent. He had a long scar running down his left cheek and eyes that looked as if they'd witnessed a lifetime of fighting.

At first, he simply flipped through the file. "You have one chance to look at it and then it gets put away. My advice is to commit as much of it to memory as possible," said Tyler sitting down on the couch next to his friend.

The voice from above spoke again. "As you can see, the target is Roberto Mallarino, in Colombia, South America. He is a known drug smuggler. He is responsible for killing hundreds of thousands of people who used heroin cut with carfentanyl. We don't typically go after drug smugglers, but this particular one clearly understood that using the carfentanyl would result in the deaths of many people. We also have clear information that he himself–and his crew–are responsible for adding carfentanyl to the drugs before they come into the United States. He buys from the main growers and suppliers in the local area. Then he cuts it, increases his profit, and sells it out of Miami and some European cities. The addicts don't care that so many people die from it. They think they can just use less to get high."

"What is this carfentanyl shit?"

"In short it is a death sentence, most of the time," the voice from above called out. "Some people call it elephant heroin. It is 10,000 times stronger than morphine. When this junk is found in drug supplies they call in hazmat teams to deal with it because it can be absorbed through the skin. Normally Narcan is the thing that keeps opioid over dosers alive, but with carfentanyl it hardly works at all. The doctors have to use large doses of Narcan if they even get to see the patient in time. This stuff is a killing machine."

Falau read through the pages, taking in as much information as possible. "My God, this guy is sick. The beheadings, mutilations, attacks on families, killing children and the elderly. Seems like there is nothing this guy won't do."

Tyler shifted and turned toward his friend. "They call him El Carnicero, which translates into The Butcher. It was a nickname that he picked up from the local police down in Columbia. They called him that because when they went to the scenes after his attacks the men said it looked a lot like a butcher's shop after they'd just dissected an animal. There was always blood and body parts everywhere. This guy knows how to send a message to everybody in the community, and all his competitors. You're just going to buy from him, or you are going to die."

"The worst part is that he had been captured and held. The United States demanded him to be extradited from Colombia, but they refused to send him. Power of the drug cartels got to too many people on the inside, and they threatened their families if they didn't keep The Butcher from being sent to the States. So now he is back on the street doing what he has always done without any punishment at all. At this point he feels unstoppable, now he has this kind of backing," said the voice from above.

"The judges want this guy alive. They want to see what he has to say and then figure out what should be done," stated Tyler.

"Do you realize what you're asking me? You act like it's no big deal! You want me to go in and infiltrate a drug smuggling operation and then bring the guy back to the United States alive. Oh, and the guy's called The Butcher! The man is a horrific murderer, and you just want me to grab him and pop him on a plane and fly back here to the States? Maybe while I'm at it you should have me capture a unicorn. Anything else that's completely impossible you want me to do?"

"We will give you your full choice of your own supplies, and Tyler can help. You know what he can produce for you. Maybe a few gadgets that can help you out."

Shaking his head back and forth, Falau looked over at Tyler as if to say, 'this is all crazy'.

"Mr. Falau, the time to answer is now. Are you in or are you out?"

Chapter 7

Sitting on board the 747 flying at 35,000 feet, Falau's fingers turned white as he gripped tightly to the armrest. For a man who didn't enjoy flying in the slightest, sitting in coach packed amongst the travelers, the smells of their bodies and their crying kids was almost too unbearable. To make all that worse, he was wedged in the middle seat with a man to his left he was sure was trying to break the record for loudest snoring, and to his right an overweight gentleman in an oversized cowboy hat. The fat man's belly hung over the armrest, not allowing any room for Falau to put his arm down. He spent the whole flight with one hand on his lap and the other one holding the armrest tight, each set of turbulence causing him to gasp and sweat even harder.

"Hello ladies and gentlemen, this is your captain John Sterling speaking. As you may have felt by now, we're hitting some turbulence, but that's to be expected. If you can all try and stay in your seats most of the flight, we can avoid any injuries resulting from more unexpected turbulence. There is no need to put on your seatbelt at this time, so try to sit back and enjoy the flight."

But no sooner had the captain's voice stopped than another abrupt bout of turbulence hit the plane, jostling it from side to side. Falau shook in the seat and bumped against the fat man's body. His breath quickened and he gasped for air, alerting those around him of his nervousness and stress.

"You okay, Hoss?" asked the fat man in the cowboy hat. A soothing drawl rolled in his speech as if he wasn't even aware of the turbulence.

"Yeah. Just a bad flyer. Never been very good at this at all."

The fat man reached out his hand for Falau to shake it and introduced himself as Billy Ray Johnson. "I'm in coffee products. I sell everything to do with them, so heading down to Columbia's nothing new for me," said the big man with a southern accent. More turbulence rocked the plane hard, pushing him hard into the cowboy's belly. Realizing that he had been holding the man's hand for far too long, he quickly removed it.

"Hey buddy don't worry about it, this happens to a lot of people. I fly this route all the time and its constant turbulence. We will be okay, don't worry about that."

"I don't understand planes. It seems to defy all logic and physics to me. No matter how many times people tell me how it works, it just doesn't make sense," said Falau, trying to get a small laugh from the big man.

With great effort, the fat man wiggled his way out of his seat and stood up in the aisle. Leaning into Falau he reached into his coat pocket he pulled out what appeared to be a small MP3 player and some headphones. "Maybe you should listen to this. I think it will help you a lot."

The cowboy made his way to the back of the plane and out of sight of Falau, who was left holding the gift. Again, the turbulence hit, but in a twist the aircraft moved up and down rather than side to side. Falau felt himself completely raise out of the seat and hit down hard. In an act of desperation, his hands fumbled around the headphones and he shoved them on his head. At this point he was willing to do anything try to make the flight easier on his stress levels. As the sweat ran down his temples the sound of classical music started. The smooth sound of the piano and gentle violins played in his ears, and he was sure that the big man knew exactly what he was talking about as he immediately started to relax.

As the music played Falau felt himself dipping into sleep. Tyler's voice gently entered his ears as if he was a DJ announcing the next song with the music behind him.

"Hey there, friend. I see that you've met my cowboy buddy. He's a good guy. Knowing how hard flying was for you, he gave you this gift." Tyler's voice fell quite over the next few seconds but the beautiful music playing had Falau picturing Tyler in his mind's eyes, though he could still feel himself falling into a deeper sleep. This was no doubt one of Tyler's inventions that he'd developed just for Falau on this flight.

"This message can only be listened to once, and then never again. It will self-erase. Falau, you're going to meet with a contact. The name of the contact is Vick, and when the time is right Vick will contact you, and it will be unmistakable."

Falau could feel himself drifting into a deeper and deeper sleep but still was able to retain everything Tyler was saying. The mad genius still had all the skills Falau had known from long before. He could create and develop things that no one else could in an incredibly short amount of time. Tyler's words were embedding deep into his mind without Falau making any effort to make it happen.

"At this point, and we must make some of this quick, sleep should start setting in and you won't be waking up until you're close to the airport. I have a couple of fun things the you might enjoy on your mission," said Tyler with obvious enthusiasm dripping from every word. He seemed unable to contain himself about what he was about to tell Falau. "So, we set you up with clothing to wear on your flight down there. Of course, the clothing isn't going to be just normal clothing. The belt you have on, the leather jacket, the collar on your shirt, are all things that can help you. First off, your belt. It's really a very simple design. It's a homing beacon. If at any time you get distressed, to the point where you can't get out and you need some back up, squeeze the belt buckle as hard as you can. It will start a reaction that will deploy people to your location and help you get out of there as fast as possible. I warn you to only use this in the most extreme of circumstances, as it will blow our cover. There's no way that you can activate the homing beacon and expect we could ever go back and attempt to pick up a target after this is been done. The next wonderful little thing you have is the leather jacket you have on. It's bulletproof. I know you're thinking that it fits well and it's comfortable and flexible, probably even the best jacket you've ever owned. What's more, if someone fired an M-16 at you from close range, all you would suffer is a bad bruise on your body. The bullet would not get through in any way. Granted that will not protect your head if they should hit you there. Your brains would just splatter in an instant, so at least it would be quick. Next the collar on your shirt. Inside the collar you'll feel something that feels like two plastic tabs. But they're not. On the right side, if you pull up the tab there is a small injection needle. This will knock anyone out for several hours. It is a one time only use device. The collar on the left side that, well that can be pulled out and used as a razor blade for combat or any other situation you might need."

Turbulence hit the plane again, jostling Falau about, but now he didn't have a care in the world. He was drifting to the sounds of music and gently riding the wave of the violence from the turbulence while listening to the soothing sound of Tyler's voice and feeling more at ease with every word his friend said.

"Your contact Vick is an insider, and is one of the best people we have. You can learn a lot. You're going to want to keep your mouth closed and take in every bit of information. Remember you're a first timer!"

All the snoring of the man next to him no longer bothered Falau, and all the turbulence seemed to no longer have any effect on him. And he felt that the best part about it was at some level he was conscious enough to understand what Tyler did for him, and all the instructions he was being given.

Tyler's voice continued. "When you land, make your way to the hotel we told you about. People will want to know what you're doing there. Columbia takes new businessman coming in very seriously. They are going to wonder what you are all about, because they keep a sharp eye out for anybody they think might be involved in the drug trade. Well it seems like you're about to fall into the deepest sleep that you've ever had in your life. You're going to wake up rested, alert, and ready to go. I have total confidence in you. I know what you can do and I know you're the right man for the job. Good night, Falau, and good luck."

Falau's eyes closed and he drifted between consciousness and deep sleep. The music continued but Tyler's voice was gone, as if it had all been a dream.

Chapter 8

The captain's voice crackled through the airplane's old public-address system.

"Ladies and gentlemen, can you please return to your seats and return your tray tables into their locked and upright positions. Please also put on your seatbelt. We will be landing at El Dorado International Airport in Bogotá, Colombia in just a few moments."

Falau saw the ground approaching quickly, and fearing somehow the aircraft would get out of control and crash to the ground was too much.

Best thing I can do is keep my eyes straightforward while the plane settles down, thought Falau.

He looked about the aircraft, trying to find the cowboy as he wanted to thank him for the gift he had given him, but the big man was nowhere to be seen, not even the massive cowboy hat. A man that large is too difficult to hide from site. How can a man that big simply disappear on an airplane at 35,000 feet?

As the plane made its final approach the Captain came over the public address system again. "Ladies and gentlemen, your Captain again with a few pieces of information that may come in handy to you. Bogotá currently has a temperature 65°F. There are mostly cloudy skies with sunshine peaking through. It looks like a beautiful day Columbian day. We are on our final approach. Please stay in your seats and refrain from walking about the cabin for your safety. Have a good day, and thank for flying Copa Airlines."

Within five minutes the plane touched down on the runway, Falau's heavy breathing finally calming down. The last five minutes had felt like an hour as he felt as if the plane was falling rather than landing. The touchdown of the wheel had made him jump in his seat, but also brought with it a wave of relief that he was back on terra firma.

The Pilot edged plane to the terminal and rolled to a stop. The jet way inched across and the seatbelt light turned off. At once everyone sprang from their seats, reaching up and pulling their carry-on luggage from the overhead compartments. They then all pushed and shoved to gain one spot ahead in the line of people waiting to disembark the plane. Staying in his seat, Falau always wondered why people worked so hard just to get one or two spots ahead in the line. Once out in the terminal it would make no difference, but people always needed that little victory in some way.

Falau secured his bag tightly behind his back. He was sure from Tyler's briefing that photographs would be taken of him from the moment he landed. Security would have the manifest of the plane and any outsiders would be processed through the security check list. There was no doubt that someone out there had eyes on him right now.

The photographs would upload directly into the computer system. Facial recognition would check every person that arrived on every fight, all faces checked against the database with all the security systems, both nationally and internationally. If a person had so much as a parking ticket the Colombian government would know about it in less than 5 minutes.

Fully aware that by this point they were watching him, Falau made his way off the jet way and into the terminal. Walking straight for the new arrivals customs area, a young man stepped in front of him holding out his hand.

“Sir, do you speak English?"

"Yes," said Falau.

"Sorry to stop you, but you have been randomly select for a baggage check. I hope you understand this is standard protocol, and you are just the person that randomly came up. We have no reason to suspect you of any wrong doing. We will try to complete this as fast as possible," said the young man in uniform.

Falau rolled his eyes, keeping in disguise, playing the part of the frustrated traveler.

“I have been through this numerous times. I understand," said Falau.

Falau slid his hands in his pockets, looking at his bags and back at the officer. Giving him, ‘the look’ did not appear to speed anything up, despite Falau's obvious frustration. Making eye contact back with Falau, the official slowed his speed in response to the attitude of the American.

The two walked over to a table set against a wall just to the side of the main area. Falau placed the bag onto the table.

The official stared into the open bag. "Do you have anything to be declare?"

"No."

"Are you transporting anything that the country of Columbia would find illegal?"

"No. Not to my knowledge. Feel free to check everything if you like," Falau said, lacing his words with sarcasm and disgust.

"Sir, you do understand how long I could make this search go on for, don't you?"

"Yes, I do. Sorry. It was a long flight."

"Understood, Sir. May I have your passport?"

Looking through the passport and checking each detail, Falau was sure that if anything was slightly out of place he would be directly on a flight back to the United States.

"Your papers say you're in farming equipment. Seems like a waste of time if you ask me. We have more than enough farming supply companies here in Colombia. Who would ever want a product from the United States when you can get one here?" asked the officer, jabbing at Falau.

Falau just smiled and nodded his head. He knew exactly what the official was trying to do, but he was not going to take the bait and resisted the temptation to reply.

A higher-ranking officer walked over to them, a variety of ranking bars across the shoulders of his uniform. He looked to be in his fifties and did not make any eye contact with Falau. He leaned into the young man in the uniform and whispered in his ear, changing the expression on the young man's face.

The officer, suddenly sounding more official, stated, "Your itinerary please."

Falau reached into his jacket pocket and pulled out two pieces of paper bound together and handed them to the young man. He checked the papers closely and then photographed them. Handing them back to Falau, he started at the big man.

"I hope you enjoy your stay here in Colombia. You are free to go," said the young man abruptly.

Gathering his things, he slid to the end of the table and pulled them into his arms. Walking and repacking his case at the same time, he knew that he was now on their radar and he had not even made it out of customs yet.

Chapter 9

Feeding the passkey into the slot in the door, the light turned green and he pushed the door open to his room at the Bogotá Hilton. Like so many of the other big hotel chains, the room was plain and simple. A large queen-size bed sat in the middle of the room. The desk and chair were along the far wall. Beside the large double sized window sat a small table and more comfortable-looking chairs.

Placing his bags on the table he examined the room, doubting they had time to get inside and add surveillance. He knew he could not fully examine things or he would blow his cover if they were watching from inside the room. *Better to keep playing the part given to him by Tyler*, he thought.

The big man walked to the bathroom to splash water on his face. Wiping himself off with the towel, he stared at himself beneath the strong lights of the mirror. It had been a long-time since he had seen himself in this kind of light. He had aged, and it had snuck up on him. He had deep lines running down his face like men twice his age. He looked unkempt, despite the suit. He was miles away from the man he wanted to be.

"You killed me. It was your fault," said the woman in the back of his mind without warning.

Attempting to fend off the flashbacks, he ran the cold water and rubbed it on his face and in his hair, hoping the shock of the cold would do the trick. He pushed his hair back with the flat of his hand and walked quickly to the main room.

He opened the mini bar like a man on a mission and grabbed two nips from it. Not even waiting to see what they were, he poured them into a glass that sat on the table and took a long sip of the concoction. It went down hard and stung his throat, but it would do the job.

Sitting down in one of the more comfortable chairs he pulled another over to place his feet on. Staring out the window he took another drink while enjoying the skyline. In the distance several tall buildings stood out. One building had a light flashing from one window, but there was no way that the swift on-off, on-off was just someone turning a room light on and off, or some kids playing. This light was focused and directed. Studying it there didn't seem to be any pattern to it. It simply flashed for short and long periods of time, but nothing over 5 seconds.

Hitting to the bottom of his drink Falau wondered who was flashing the light and for what purpose. *Could it be Vick?* he thought.

Like a lightning bolt from the blue he finally realized what the light was doing. It was Morse code. He recognized it from his short time in the military. Falau smiled and grabbed the paper and pencil from the desk. *It could be just some kids having fun*, he thought, but better to know what he was dealing with.

Copying down the dots and dashes of light he kept going until the sequence had repeated itself twice. Opening his smart phone, he deciphered the message and knew from the few simple words it said that it was from Vick.

"Corner of Carrera 9 and Calle 73. Tyler."

Tyler's name was all the big man needed to grab his coat and rush out the door.

Chapter 10

The ash on the cigarette had grown long as it sat on its perch in the groove of the ashtray. The owner had somehow forgotten about it despite the constant stream of smoke drifting up from his desk.

Behind the desk sat a young man in his 20s. His olive skin and dark hair were not enough to charm ladies, so he focused his attention on his studies and work. That kind of dedication led him directly to the National Police of Colombia, straight out of university. And within a few short years the whiz kid had risen to the rank of lieutenant in the Special Operations Commandos. The SOC was tasked with being sent into action in situations considered high-risk tasks. But now he was stuck. The only way to move up the ladder was to have someone die above him, or to create a giant splash to draw positive attention onto himself. Regardless, neither of those seemed particularly possible as he sat in a one-window office at the city airport.

Carlos Rivera flipped through the hundreds of photographs that lined his desk, all taken by the facial recognition software at the security area for incoming international travelers. Rivera felt like he had been tasked to find a needle in a haystack. Thousands of people each day entered the country through the airport, and it was his job to pick out the person that did not belong. When he volunteered to work on the drug task force, he never thought it would involve sitting behind a desk at the airport. He was assured he had a very important job and if he screwed up on the task, he knew it would be his job.

Going through the photos for the third time, he was again taken aback by the American with a hardened face who had been detained but cleared to go on. The leadership felt he posed no threat and was ill-equipped to provide any kind of smuggling operation for the locals in that line of business. But Rivera remained uneasy with the man named Falau.

Turning to the computer where he had accessed the video, he scrolled to the moment when Falau was in the security area. Studying the man, he seemed oddly out of place. He was glancing to the side when he felt he was not being watched, a sign of a man who knew what he was doing. He didn't overplay his hand, but rather took sneaky looks to gauge the room, rather than someone looking to see if they were being surrounded. That is what normal passengers would do in that situation. Rivera remembered the words of his old trainer from years ago: *when people get detained they get claustrophobic. They feel like they're being held in. Watch out for the fight or flight response.* This man Falau showed none of that.

Flicking through the papers the National Policeman found Falau's itinerary and scanned it. In no location did it show a clear meeting with any of the local coffee growers. Rivera knew that if this man was here for anything to do with farming, that his contacts would surely be within the drug trade.

This was exactly the kind of bust he had been waiting for–the one that slipped by the others–and he would pounce on it. All his life Rivera had wanted to exact revenge on the local drug cartel and its leader, The Butcher.

Rivera straightened himself up in his chair, remembering back to his childhood and the moment he learned how The Butcher had killed his brother, who'd been dealing drugs in the streets. They refused to give up their money to The Butcher, so he responded by hanging them alive in the town square. He jammed a spike into their lower backs, up under their skin, and out through their necks. The brothers lived for several agonizing hours, but the community was too afraid to get involved for fear The Butcher would go after them. The ends of the poles were dug into the ground to put them on display for all to see. It was such a horrific sight that Carlos's parents would not let him see, but he had heard the stories around the neighborhood in all the graphic detail, painting an image he could never wipe from his mind.

Carlos knew that arresting Falau would disrupt The Butcher's operation and he'd get a minimal amount of revenge for the loss of his brother.

Looking back to the itinerary, the name Hilton stood out. *Carlos smiled. Hope you have a nice sleep, Mr. Falau, because I am going to be with you for the rest of your trip,* he thought, tapping on the picture.

Rivera stood up from his desk and grabbed his keys. Moving to the door he put his leather jacket on and took his motorcycle helmet from a hook on the door. Closing the door behind him Rivera knew this could be his one shot to advance himself in the eyes of the leaders of the National Police of Colombia.

Chapter 11

Walking through the front door of the hotel and onto the street, a gust of wind hit Falau, making 65° feel more like 50°. The busy street was alive with cars and pedestrians moving in every which direction. Most pedestrians wore thick coats with their collars up to keep the wind at bay. Falau looked over the crowd, knowing this was making his job more difficult... high collars concealed faces and was good for covering people's eyes. The street looked like a mass of black jackets with only tops of heads sticking out of them.

He moved down the steps and onto the sidewalk. Pushing his hands into his pockets, he hunched up his shoulders and started to walk at a casual pace. Being followed would be the worst thing that could happen now. He attempted to dance a fine line between walking too fast and trying not to appear too slow. Spotting a tail would be much harder on foot with so many people around. He knew any number of people could be going where he was just by chance.

Staring into a store window, he used it to check the reflection across the street. Everyone seemed to keep moving. Nobody even looked over. Opening his phone, he held it to his ear and began to speak.

"I know you want me to get the coat, but I have no idea what more you want," Falau snapped into the phone to nobody. Continuing to argue, he turned side-to-side constantly while talking and taking video with the phone.

"You want it so bad, just get the damn coat yourself... anything I get will just be a waste of time."

Turning the phone off Falau was sure he had captured on video all the people that had been around him and in the area. Pushing the shop door open he went inside and headed straight for the women's coats.

"Can I help you, Sir?" asked an effeminate clerk as he strolled over to Falau. "I can see you have good taste. Are you shopping for your wife?"

"Actually, I am getting some pictures of different styles, then she can get an idea of them and we can come back and pick it out. You know, saves me from having to be here if she tries on thirty different styles."

The clerk smiled and nodded at Falau with a good amount of condescension towards the fashion impaired American. "Well, if she likes one please send her to us and we will take good care of her."

"Thanks," said the big man as the clerk strolled away.

Taking out his phone Falau turned down the volume and started to watch the video while pulling out different coats and acting like he was taking photographs. The faces all seemed normal. If he was being followed, the guy was very good and was not tipping his hand. *Am I just paranoid?* thought Falau. *Who the hell even knows I'm here?*

Getting back out onto the street he kept his pace steady and even, stopping at the occasional shop to look inside the window keeping up his façade. Passing the Universidad Santo Tomás he got to the intersection of Carrera 9 and Calle 73. There was a beehive of activity: taxis going up to the sidewalks and people hopping in. People cutting across the street against the lights. The screech of brakes from a driver who had not been watching where he was going. It was organized chaos at its finest. A kind of ballet, where all the dancers were moving on their own to different styles of music. It was just a matter of time until two crashed into one another.

A car screeched to a halt in front of Falau. A taxi sign adorned the top of the car and it was clear this was a bootleg taxi, as nothing indicated it was part of one of the big companies working the streets. Falau knew these guys always worked harder to get their fares and had to stay one step ahead of the law. Normally they were also a bit riskier than the normal taxi because they were operating on the wrong side of the law. The driver leaned over, pulling down the window. "Need a lift?"

Staring into the car Falau saw a woman driving. She was attractive, with dark hair and blue eyes. Despite seeing none of her skin other than her face Falau could see she was strong and fit, and seemed to be the kind of woman that could handle herself in a fight with a man.

"You need a ride or what, Mister? Tyler said you might need a ride."

Hearing Tyler's name was all Falau needed to take this ride from a stranger. If she were working for someone after him then they had done their homework alau reached down to open the door with a loud creak and hopped into the ack seat. No sooner had Falau hit the seat than the woman screeched away om the curb and burst into the middle of the intersection. Heading next to a de street, the tires squealed on the turn.

"Did Tyler teach you how to drive?" snapped Falau, but it was met with si-nce from the woman. Again and again Falau attempted to engage the woman ith some kind of conversation, but was constantly met with no response.

"Can you speak?" Falau asked her with sarcasm and building frustration.

"Yeah. Shut up," said the woman, letting Falau know exactly where he stood ith her.

Cutting the wheel hard again she pulled into a taxi parking garage. Keeping er speed up she raced to the far end of the garage and pulled into the spot next several other cars that looked exactly like the one she was driving.

"Out! Now! Follow me and shut up!" demanded the woman, not waiting r Falau to answer. The door swung open and she started to walk away, causing alau to scramble to catch up to her.

The sudden sound of more tires screeching made Falau look back. The car as being driven away by a woman with dark hair and a man in the backseat. he had thought of everything to keep the cover alive, just in case they were be-g watched. Falau was sure that by the time they had hit the garage entrance e man would have on clothing similar to his and nobody would know the dif-rence. The woman continued to move at a swift pace as they exited out the ack of the garage. Reaching down to grab Falau by the hand, she dropped back ext to him giving the appearance that the two were a couple.

"This is all very sudden. I don't even know your name," said Falau sarcasti-lly.

"Don't flatter yourself," said the woman, smiling and leading him to the or of the building next to the garage. She then unlocked the door to the artment building and went inside. Rushing up one flight of steps she led em into the hall and to the first door on the right. Apartment 2J. Unlocking e door they went in. All Falau knew was this woman knew Tyler's name, and thing more. He wondered if he'd just walked into an ambush following noth-g more than the name of a friend.

Falau closed the door behind him, and across the room the woman closed e curtain. Turning back to him, the two measured each other up.

"My name is Carla Romero, but my friends call me Vick."

"You're Vick?" questioned Falau, his forehead furrowing as he shook his head. "Sorry, I was expecting someone a little more... a man."

"I get that a lot. Guess the name does its job as a disguise. So, you're the guy they sent to get The Butcher. You must be some kind of a badass, right. Ex-CIA? FBI? Navy seal?"

"Nothing like that. I just needed a job."

"Just needed a job?" Carla raised her eyebrows. "Okay, I understand the need to keep things close to the vest. I respect that."

Falau smiled and walked over to the window and peeked out the curtain.

"So, Falau, my job is to give you all the info I have so you can take down The Butcher. You need to listen up, because this guy is not just a sick son of a bitch, but he is smart. Really smart. As a kid he could've gone to any university he liked, but he didn't see the sense in going to school where he knew more than the professors. He wanted to pull his family out of poverty, so he looked to drugs. He is so smart he knows not to be the top man. The Police always want to get the top man. It is a better show for the cameras. He knows that it is a lot better to be down the line. You can keep low, and still make millions of dollars It has only been the last few years he turned into The Butcher. His brother stole a million dollars from him and put out a hit on him, looking to take over the operation. He felt he needed to send a message to everyone who might think he was weak. So, he paid the zookeepers not to feed the lions for two weeks. He then dragged his brother into the zoo with the help of a few men. Then they threw him to the lions in the middle of the day. Families were there. School children were there. Story has it, they even put blood in his hair to get the lions to attack. He is not a nice guy at all."

"Well I wasn't thinking of taking him out for coffee. I just want to get him and bring him back," said Falau. "Where is he?"

The woman sat on the sofa and grabbed the top of the coffee table and opened it like a car hood, exposing several handguns hidden inside. "I prefe the 9 mm, but most guys like to brag about having the big one, so here's a .4 for you."

Falau smirked at Carla's ribbing. The more he spoke with her the more he liked her. She gave as good as she got. She was a fighter, but still maintaine her feminine side through it all. There was nothing overly masculine about he but her ability to take care of any situation in front of her was undeniable, even without having seen it.

"As I'm sure you know he runs drugs up to Miami and other spots on the east coast of North America and some places in Europe. Miami is the easiest because he could always fall back into Cuba if things got messy with the Coast Guard. He does it all through a warehouse over at the import/export station here in the city. He has everyone paid off so it is easy to hide drugs. He has at least thirty men working for him at the warehouse and on the street. The most notice you will ever have before they know he's gone is about two hours. If they can't find him for that long they will be looking for him."

"Thanks for the info. What is the address of the warehouse?" asked Falau

"I will show you."

"Sorry, but I work alone. This is my mission," interrupted Falau.

"Mr. Falau, I'm coming with you. I want this guy nailed just like you, and I'm going to help. Besides there's no way in the world you're getting into that warehouse without me. They will see you coming a mile away," she replied, smiling the smile of a person who knows they are right.

Falau looked to the ground, shook his head and wiped his face with his hand. "Okay, but I'm the lead. You fall in with my orders and no other way around it. You got it?"

"Sir. Yes Sir," quipped the woman Falau could not help but like.

Chapter 12

As day turned to night Falau and Carla drove down a side street and pulled to the side of the road under trees that hung over the car. A street light flickered on and off about 10 feet behind them and most of the light from the main roads was muted on their quiet street.

Cracking the driver side window, a sudden cool breeze caused Falau to tighten up his coat as they sat side by side watching the end of the street.

The activity in the warehouse was constant. People coming and going in all areas. Several forklifts moving pallets of merchandise to various locations. There was a large chain-link fence around the property and there was only one gate in and out.

"Tyler gave me something he said you would like," Carla said, reaching into the inside pocket of her jacket. "If these things really work it will be true what they say about him."

"What? That he is a genius?"

Carla turned her head to Falau with a look of total confusion on her face "You know about that?"

"Tyler and I go way back. I know what he's capable of," said Falau, not look ing away from the warehouse.

Carla produced a square piece of what look like cellophane and pulled i into two pieces. Leaning toward the windshield, she pressed one piece in fron of herself and one piece in front of Falau.

"Look straight into it," she said, gazing into the new addition to the win dow.

"Oh, I'll be damned. Binoculars made from cellophane!" exclaimed Fala trying to make sense of how Tyler could create something like that.

"This defies everything I know about magnification and how it works," said a stunned Carla.

The two partners resumed watching the goings on with different workers at the warehouse and what tracks they were taking as they went to and from the building. Looking for a pattern in the chaos of what they did was a tall task.

"That's him," said a cold and detached Carla. "The one inside the guard shack at the entrance to the warehouse."

Adjusting his eyes Falau drew his attention to the man he felt looked different than the picture he'd seen of him. He looked harder and more aggressive. A deep scar ran down his right cheek. Jagged and deep, it was clear it had not been treated properly in a hospital. It may not have ever been stitched up. His goatee was unkempt and hanging low, 6-inches at least from his chin. A cigarette dangled from his mouth, glowing bright orange every few moments when he took a drag from it. He was the alpha male of the group, there was no doubt about that. Falau watched as the others change their course so as to not converge with him or get into his line of sight. Word was spreading fast with the outside workers that The Butcher was at the door.

Without looking away Falau tapped on the steering wheel. "Looks like a tough guy. He could be problematic down the road. When should we hit him?"

"This place has no slow time. Anytime is good as any other. We just have to get him alone," replied Carla.

Turning his head, he saw her sitting with her back against the passenger side door, and without warning his mind flashed, causing him to gasp for breath.

The beautiful woman from the flashback was now mixed with Carla. Falau's mind drifted between them, overlapping them, and blood started dripping down from Carla's hairline and covering her face. Shards of glass sprung up on her cheeks and her forhead. The light left her eyes and her mouth dropped open. "You killed me," she said, "It was your fault. The light was red. You know the light was red. You killed me." The words came out of Carla's mouth but it was not her voice. It was the voice of the other woman.

Falau's mind suddenly jerked back to the present. Sweat ran off his face. His hand gripped the steering wheel hard and he had an overwhelming urge to run away.

"No. No. No!" snapped Falau at the images in his head, overrun by the evil that had taken up residence in his mind. A hand grabbed his and pulled it away from the keys before he turned the engine over.

"What are you doing?" asked Carl.

"I didn't kill you!! It isn't my fault!" barked the terrified man.

"Falau! You okay? Falau!" Placing her hand on his face she pulled his eyes toward her. They were out of focus and looked right through the young woman. "Falau!"

"Yeah! What? I'm good now!" yammered the big man as he dropped back into the present, unable and unwilling to explain what was happening to him. "Sorry, I was just thinking about the car accident a long time ago."

"I understand. Some things never go away. You can live them over and over again like they're happening for the first time right in front of you," sympathized Carla, and Falau immediately sensed a kinship with the woman he had only met a short time ago. He could tell from her voice that she understood about the flashbacks and how anyone could fall into them without warning.

"I call it my dark half. It pops up occasionally. I manage it the best I can."

"Your dark half? I like that. I have one of those two. I remember my brothers being killed. Every sound, every look from other people, every smell in the air. They were slaughtered like dogs for no good reason. Each was given a Colombian necktie. Do you know what that is?" asked Carla, her eyes drifting away from Falau. He could feel her pain with each word, knowing she too was seeing everything she said in her mind's eye.

"No"

"You see, if they think you're a snitch or you're really pissing people off they give you a Colombian necktie. They cut your throat so deep that it cuts into your windpipe. Then they reach up and pull your tongue out through the hole. Sends a message to everyone what they will do to you if you cross them. But for a kid to see your brothers like that causes something to be taken from you soul. Something that you can never get back. I walked out of the door to go to school, and found my two brothers with the Colombian neckties impaled on the rod-iron fence at the front of the house. You stop being a kid right then and there. I didn't scream and I didn't cry. I just got angry."

Looking out into the distance Falau searched for the right words to say. It was clear her pain was equal in every way to his. She just managed to use it as fu el to go after the killer. She wanted revenge for what The Butcher did. Falau felt a stream of shame run over him for not having the resolve that Carla showed. He had fallen into a shell and hid from the world after his trauma. He'd gained nothing, and had not grown at all from it. He simply gave up on life and was willing and waiting to die.

"My brothers were good guys. There was no way they were into anything like drug running. They had a future without any of that."

"Did Carlos kill them?" inquired Falau.

"No. But he gave the order. Nobody kills anyone in the city without him giving the order first."

"I'm sorry you had to deal with that. It's not fair."

"Thank you. That's why this one is so important to me. I need to take this guy down hard. I thought we had him in the trial but he has too much money and too much power over the government. Now we get revenge and justice my way."

"I'm happy to help you in any way I can. I think it's time we take a walk and get a closer look at things, and see if we can find a way to pay The Butcher a little visit," said Falau with a hard look on his face.

"Let's go," responded the woman who had only justice on her mind.

Chapter 13

The leather clad man backed into the shelter of the tree. Rivera sat on a stone wall in the shadows just 10-feet from his Yamaha YZF R6 motorcycle, a bike built for speed and precision. People passed by barely glancing at the man smoking a cigarette and dressed in leather riding gear.

Rivera thought about the couple that sat in the car two blocks away from him. Questions came to mind without answers. Who was the woman? Why were they watching the warehouse? What happened to the cab they were in?

The questions kept coming, but he knew he was lucky to even know where they were. If not for the closed-circuit TV cameras based around the city he would've never seen Falau leave the hotel to get picked up by the woman. She had to be part of the drug smuggling ring. It was the only thing that made any sense to Rivera. Rivera searched his mind as he watched the woman in the car reach across and take the man's face into her hand. *They must be using farming equipment to move the drugs. Maybe they load the equipment in the fields and then move the equipment back to the transport area? Then the guy Falau goes home saying no sale with equipment filled with drugs?*

The car door swung open, causing Rivera to drop his cigarette. He held back against the wall trying not to reveal himself. The woman and the man got out and moved onto the sidewalk.

The couple started walking up the street about a couple of feet apart. Their demeanor made it clear they were just business partners.

Rivera hopped on his motorcycle and put on his helmet. Turning the key the bike came to life. Getting involved without official permission from the Commandos of the National Police was something clearly he knew could back fire on him, but if he was ever going to push his name to the top of the list this just might be the case to do it. He was willing to take the chance to get the big payoff.

Rivera pushed the bike up to its normal speed until he was within 20-feet of his targets. He revved the engine and popped the clutch, causing the bike to chirp its tires and lurch forward. Instinctively the couple looked as he raced past them.

There was no doubt it was Falau and the woman. Now the question was, what were they doing outside the warehouse if they were part of the smuggling operation?

Approaching the corner Rivera slowed down and took a right, and once out of eyesight of the couple he pumped his fist in excitement.

Chapter 14

A motorcycle sped past them in a commotion of sound and speed.

"Stupid kid," Falau said, annoyed.

They continued walking up the street while attempting to pass as lovers. Falau reached down and took Carla's hand, and held it tight in his own. Still focusing her gaze up the street she questioned him. "What is this all about?"

"No man would walk the street with a woman that looks as good as you without making sure everyone knew she was taken. I'm just completing the disguise."

Carla laughed softly. "Really? How nice to know you think I'm attractive. I was beginning to think you were dead inside."

"It's obvious," Falau said, teasing, "just like it's obvious that I'm extremely attractive. No need to agree. Like I said, it's obvious."

Carla let out another laugh she knew was far too loud and would draw attention if anyone heard it. The couple was now less than a block away from th warehouse and its high chain link fence.

"To make this more believable, just in case anyone is watching, we may a well do this thing right."

Taking a step-in front of the big man, she stopped him in his tracks. Pullin herself in close to him she looks deep into his eyes. "Put your hands on my hips, she whispered and Falau did as he was instructed.

Pulling herself up–and Falau down–she kissed him gently on the lips an then lowered herself into a hug, dropping her face against his chest.

Falau held his breath, absorbing all the affection he could. Despite knowin this was all part of a cover he could not help but enjoy the feeling of her touc It'd been years since anyone had touched him with such affection.

Carla pulled back and put her arms around Falau's waist, and he followed her lead doing the same. Without warning she slid her hand into the back pocket of his jeans, catching Falau off guard.

"This is what makes it really believable," she said while squeezing his buttocks.

Falau chuckled while looking down at what he now considered a new friend. Her humor and skill was all he needed to enjoy her.

The two got closer to the corner and rounded to the right. Continuing their giggling and the sounds of a couple in love, they walked unnoticed 200 yards from the entrance to the facility. At this distance, the security lights got more intense and they were able to make out the staff clearly. Another hundred yards down the street and the property of the facility ended with a road that turned into the left amid more chain-link fence.

"No cameras," commented Falau. "I would have thought that an important building containing exports would be covered in heavy security."

"No need for cameras. This place is 24 hours a day, 7 days a week and 365 days a year. Cameras would just document all the illegal shit going on in here. They post this place as a government building so they can do what they want whenever they want. Government sanctioned drug smuggling brought to you by Colombia," replied Carla, trying but failing to keep her temper in check.

They moved to the side street on the left and hugged close to the fence line, searching for a place that covered by the high stacks of pallets.

"This is the spot," directed Carla, dropping to one knee where one of the support bars on the fence stood. Her hands worked quickly as she pulled away the section of wire that ran along the bottom of the fence. She had noticed that the wire had been broken at that point, most likely from a piece of equipment breaking it into two. "Pull it up for me!"

Falau again did as instructed and lifted the fence, and Carla rolled under it. Without hesitation, she stood pressing her back against the chain-link, holding it off the ground and waving Falau through. Falau dropped to the ground and rolled under the fence, and Carla put it back into position right behind him.

Behind the pallets Falau wiped the dirt and earth from his pants and shirt.

"Falau?" called to Carla in a stern whisper. "I have our targets," she said pointing to the closest side of the warehouse.

Gently, Falau moved to her position attempting to make as little noise as possible. From 50-yards away he could see two men had exited from the loading door of the warehouse. The men were of average size and appeared to be sneaking off for a cigarette break.

"They are perfect," he whispered. "We just need to be stealthy."

Carla nodded in agreement and motioned for Falau to stay where he was. As she started to move forward she felt Falau grab her arm.

"Where are you going?"

"I can take care of this."

"Sure you can, but we're a team."

"Right," she replied sarcastically. "I need you to provide cover in case things go wrong. You know, with the gun."

Trying not to reveal his embarrassment, he nodded and she was on her way. He felt as if he wanted to protect her, but was not sure why. She was more than capable by herself, and they had only just met.

Creeping ever so slowly, she moved to within 20-yards. Keeping low to the ground, she looked through the pallets and could see the men still holding their position. One dropped his cigarette and his left leg twisted to put it out. Time was short. She needed to make the move.

Reaching into her shirt she found the strap of her bra. Rolling it to the side she pulled out a small 4-inch-long tube that was not much more than a swizzle stick.

Patting the back of the tube two small darts felt into her hand. Removing the dart caps, she loaded one into the tube. Staying low to the ground she took aim at the man on the right. She took a deep breath, making sure not to have the tube in her mouth as she did, having heard far too many stories of people sucking in their own poisonous darts. The quick thrust of air and the dart rushed through the air, going through the man's pants and causing him to smack his leg like he was stung by a bee.

Wasting no time another dart was loaded and fired off, causing the same reaction from the second man.

Before the men could realize what was happening they had dropped to the ground unconscious from the rush of chemicals that entered their systems.

Falau moved forward when given the signal to move up, seeing the two men lying on the ground. "Dead?" he questioned, staring at the bodies as they lay on the ground.

"No, just gone to sleep for the next 12 hours to wake up with a hell of a headache."

Not wasting time with more chit chat with Falau, Carla made her way over to the bodies and grabbed one by the shirt, and dragged it behind the pallets. Falau helped her, once he realized what she was doing.

"Take their badges," she demanded

"Got it."

With the bodies hidden under a stack of pallets and new security credentials, the partners felt more comfortable walking in the open. The loading door was now shut and the only way into the building was the main entrance. Trying to conceal themselves, the couple kept close to the building so as not to look out of place. The closer they got to the entrance the more they allowed themselves to be seen. Now walking with purpose, the two were acting like they were in charge of the operation at the warehouse.

Stopping at the guard shack at the entrance of the warehouse, a young man sat inside listening to a baseball game in Spanish.

"ID?" he questioned, not looking away from the paperwork that sat on his desk.

Pulling the badge on the lanyard up, the man waved them through, barely glancing their way.

"Go ahead," he mumbled

Carla and Falau entered the operation with a smile. They both felt the same way. We are in!

Chapter 15

The warehouse spread out wide and high. Falau felt it looked more like an air craft hangar than the inside of a warehouse. The ceiling approached 40-fee making the main area easily able to house stacks of cars or boats. The facilit was alive with activity that showed no indication of the time of day. They ra the same way 24 hours a day.

The floor stretched out far to the right and left, and in each direction ther were rows of products waiting to be moved into the next location. At the fron of the aisle was a sign indicating the company that owned that space.

Seeing others wearing a badge the same as the ones they had on, Carl watched them question people about what was happening and then move on.

"We hit the jackpot," she said, walking with an air of confidence.

"Why?" asked Falau.

"The badges were for inspectors. They think we are here to look at the me chandise going in and out."

Falau nodded his head without changing his expression. He knew the ir spector badge was a major advantage but also knew it would not ensure the get to The Butcher or secure him for transport.

Spotting a worker who had stepped in and spoke with The Butcher at th front gate, Falau nudged Carla, showing her what he had seen but not saying word.

The worker made his way over to the sign that said, "Jetway Internationa Soon he vanished out of sight down the opening that had products stacke 20-feet high on each side.

"Exporters. Figures," remarked Carla. "Now... how do they do it? You hav to hide the drugs, but in what?"

"Anything they can get their hands on."

The two started to walk over to the Jet International location, trying to exude a sense that they were in charge of what was happening. With their heads held high, they looked about as if they were examining everything. It was clear that a conversation with the examiners was not a good thing for the workers, and could only lead to trouble for anyone of the companies operating on the warehouse.

"Jetway International is a legitimate company. They have been around since I was a kid. The company set up here in Colombia for the cheap labor, and then ship everything back to the States, Canada and Europe. I wonder if the management is in on what's happening with the drug operation?"

Falau stopped and went over to a box whose label said it held children's toys. He popped the top off the box and pulled out a baby doll and looked it over. "My guess is that they know what they are doing. I'm sure The Butcher has intimidated them to the point that they let him do whatever he wants. They keep their mouths closed, or they and their families die."

Carla rolled her eyes knowing Falau was right. The Butcher would not give up any amount of money when he could just kill–or threaten to kill–and get the same results.

As they strolled down the aisle, they saw a staggering range of products to be shipped by Jetway International. They moved everything from coffins to toys, from baby products to prosthetic limbs. Falau could envisage a way in which any of the products could be used to move drugs, and with such a large quantity of merchandise being shipped they could parcel out the drugs in small amounts over a vast number of concealed items.

"Hey! What you are doing down here? This is personnel only!" barked an overweight Colombian no more than 40-years-old. The man could not have been more average in any way. His height, complexion, and even mustache did not stand out. He did not break stride until he was within a foot of the couple.

"You two need to get out of here, right now. This is a personnel area only!" declared the man, pointing the opposite direction.

"Inspection," Falau said coldly, not making eye contact with the man but pointing to the badge that hung from his shirt. "We need to check you guys, just like every other company in the facility. Today we got stuck with you. Let's make the best of things."

"You guys must be new. We don't get inspected much. My bosses worked it out that everything gets inspected early so we can ship faster," replied the worker, trying to explain the arrangements without divulging too much information.

"That's not what we were told," Carla interjected.

"Hey lady!" said the worker. "I'm talking to the man."

Falau looked out the corner of his eyes to see the red rise up on Carla's cheeks. The worker had lit the fuse to a time bomb and he didn't even know it. Falau wanted to smile but instead he held his tongue and waited for the show to start.

"Excuse me? What did you say?" the feisty woman started with a hard edge to her words. "You listen to me. I can make your life a living hell. I can make your team unpack every single box, and you will have to layout each item so I can inspect them all personally. I can hold off everything that you have a shipment for, and put it all in quarantine for 30 days. How would your boss like that? How'd you like it if I tell him you were not following procedure and decided to insult an inspector? My guess is he wouldn't be happy. I swear to you that if you do not start giving me the respect I deserve, that my team and I will climb up your ass and inspect every inch of this place and we will shut you down for any of the smallest infractions."

The worker's eyes widened and he took a step back away from the woman who had suddenly become uncomfortably close. "Hey, I'm just doing what the boss tells me to. I'm sorry, I didn't mean to insult you."

"You should've thought about that before," she snapped, turning and walking away.

"You may want to update your resume," said Falau to the worker with the sternest look he could muster.

"Hey man. I need this job. I have a wife and kids. If I get fired she is going to kill me," pleaded the worker. Falau glanced down at him with rolling eyes.

"I'll see what I can do. She gets hot headed, but to tell you the truth I don't want to spend the next 12-hours going over all your shipments. Just lay low and I will take care of it and get her to relax."

"No problem. Just let me know if you need anything," replied the worker as he walked in the opposite direction back to the main floor.

Falau moved down the aisle quickly to reach Carla and found her paused at an open coffin on the side of the aisle.

"This is how they do it. They pack the drugs in the coffins. These are military coffins, and they have a false bottom. They put the drugs in with the dead serviceman. Nobody in customs would disturb a deceased military member. They take the drugs out of the funeral home when they get the soldier back. You can ship into any of the countries and no one will say a thing. I heard stories about them doing this years ago."

Leaning over the coffin she ran her hand on the bottom and pushed hard. A small panel opened where the deceased person's right foot would have rested. The sick contraption used for drug smuggling caused the young woman to stare blankly into it. A hand awkwardly rested on her shoulder to comfort her. Falau gave her all the comfort he dared show, unsure of how much was too much.

"That must be the office up there," he said gingerly while pointing further down the aisle. A set of wooden steps ran up to a door. "He's in there. Perfect place to make our move."

Carla nodded and she walked with quiet confidence to the steps and ascended them quickly. She knocked on the door, standing two vigilant steps to he side for fear of a burst of gunfire coming raking through the door. But the only thing they heard was a voice that said, "Come in."

Pushing open the door Falau saw two men sitting at a desk reviewing stacks of files and looking worn down from the task.

"Excuse me. We are the inspectors. Is Mr. Mallarino available?" asked Falau, attempting to sound official.

"Sorry, you just missed him. He went home but he should be back around 0am tomorrow. You want to leave a message?"

"No need. We just wanted to let him know that the inspection went fine nd he could continue as he always has. We will send in a copy of the night's eport for his files."

They backed out of the room and down the steps. Moving with purpose hey made their way to the front of the warehouse to see The Butcher pulling ut of the gate in his car. Knowing there was no way they could take him down ow the couple strolled towards the main gates watching The Butcher's tail ghts disappearing down the main street and into the distance.

Chapter 16

Dropping into the driver's seat, Carla turned the key to bring the car to life.

"Go! Go! Go!" Falau yelled.

The car screeched from the curb and raced up the street, taking a hard-right turn without slowing down. Falau was pleased to have Carla behind the wheel. She was the one who had far more skill when it came to this kind of driving.

Pulling the .45 caliber pistol from his waistband he checked the magazine to make sure it was full. "Hand me your 9mm," demanded Falau

"It's on my ankle. Just grab it."

Reaching down, Falau lifted the young woman's pant leg and spotted the gun. Taking it from its holster his hand accidentally rubbed against her skin, reminding him how long it'd been since he felt the softness of a woman.

Opening the magazine, he saw it was filled. He popped it back in anc loaded one round in the chamber. Going to the glove compartment he pullec out another magazine, quickly packing one for the 9mm and one for the 45.

"Shit, Carla!" squawked Falau as the car screeched to a harsh stop, but thei noticed her eyes were locked on the car in front of them.

"It's him," she said in a calm, soft voice. "He's looking at me in the rearviev mirror."

"Change the radio station. Play cool. Look natural."

Carla reached for the radio as the stop light turned green. The Butcher's ca pulled away with his eyes still locked on her in the rearview mirror.

"I don't like this."

"The gas. Pump it a little. Like you're drunk."

The car lurched forward, then settled down as they followed their targe from a safe distance. "It's not like he's even looking at the road," she said, a trac of fear in her voice for the first time since she and Falau had met. "His eyes are locked on the mirror, looking right at us. He must know."

"He's on high alert but he has no idea we're after him. Unless the two guys in the office called him." Falau punched the dashboard in frustration for not taking more time and care to deal with the office men.

The Butcher's car slowed at a stop light as they pulled up behind. Carla ran her hand through her hair and attempted to look like she was joking with her friend, but all the while she could see the madman looking back examining her. The hum of the motors was the only thing breaking the silence in the crisp air of the night.

The light changed to green and The Butcher pulled away slowly, still looking back at their car.

Carla followed. "He knows. I can see it in his eyes. He's checking out everything I do."

"Calm down. No need to jump the gun with a guy like this. Let him make the first move," replied Falau. Falau could feel himself starting to work off instinct. His skills with this kind of work were coming back to life, and for the first time in years he felt sure of himself and sure of what he was doing.

The Butcher slowly pulled away from them again.

"Hold steady on his speed. Let him pull away."

10, 15, 25, and now 30-feet ahead, The Butcher edged his car up to the next stop light that turned from green to yellow. He hit the intersection when it turned red and punched the gas, jerking the car forward. The sound of the engine kicking in ripped back to the couple, who saw the taillights suddenly racing into the distance as a red light stared them in the face.

"Fuck it! Go!" screamed Falau.

Pounding the gas Carla pushed the car into high gear, bursting through the traffic coming from the left and the right. Seeing The Butcher two blocks ahead nd turning right, she saw the chance to make up time, pushing the car up to 80 iles an hour on the narrow side streets. Stomping on the clutch she dropped e car into third gear and took the corner, hard trying not to fishtail. Tires creeching hard, she had gained on The Butcher.

The sheer power of Carla's Mustang made up the ground and she was suddenly within two car lengths of the madman, who was again looking in his earview mirror at her.

Falau pulled the .45 from his waistband and opened his window.

"Don't kill him!" Carla demanded looking at Falau and reaching out her arm to grab his shirt.

With her attention on Falau and off from the car in front of her The Butcher saw his opportunity and jammed on his brakes, causing his car to skid.

Carla's eyes darted back to the killer to see the blinding red tail lights shining in her face. Both her feet jammed the brakes hard into the floor, causing her own car to skid, but the momentum was too much and the car crashed into the back of The Butcher's vehicle with a horrendous crunch. Carla spun the wheel looking for any way to control their car, that had totally spun out, pushing them from the road and up onto the sidewalk.

Falau's hand moved his head after banging it hard against the dashboard, cracking the .45 handgun into his skull. Blood dripped from a cut above his hairline and he felt an immediate headache coming on. He was sure it was a concussion, but he had no time to worry about that now.

A sharp pounding sensation hit his mind hard. *It's your fault. You killed me,* echoed through his mind with flashes of his old love covered in blood and looking up at him from the well of the passenger seat.

The Butcher's car lurched to life again after bouncing off a tree and he raced up another block and drove through a gate and up a driveway. The sound of the engine roaring up the long driveway could be heard in the distance and the two pursuers tried to pull themselves together.

"It's now or never. Our cover is blown," said Falau as Carla pulled the car to the side of the road.

Wiping her hand against her mouth she inspected the blood from the now missing tooth. "I can't promise you I won't kill the son of a bitch."

"I know," replied big man, "and I understand. But if I get him I am going to bring him back."

The beautiful woman nodded her head in agreement. "Fair enough. Let's get him."

Chapter 17

ursting from the car the partners targeted the fence of The Butcher's home. heir feet smacked off the ground as they worked their way to the destination or very different reasons. No matter if it was for revenge or money, they both ad just one thing in mind, and that was capturing the madman who had irned killing and intimidation to an art form.

The fence of The Butcher's house was large and made of stone, thus easy to imb with many foot holes and grips for the hands. It was built more for aesnetic value than to keep anyone in or out. Falau crouched down and interlaced is fingers so his partner could slip her foot into them quickly to get a solid oost up the wall. He pushed her up with rapid speed, surprised at how light ne was.

Dropping to her stomach on the flat top of the wall she reached down, givg her new friend a hand and helped him up. Falau took her hand quickly, seeg her as an equal in this endeavor. Gender meant nothing to him now. She as his teammate, and despite her femininity it all left his mind now they were oth in attack mode. Carla was the same in every way to him, and he felt he'd ever had a finer partner in his life. It was clear to him that anything he could o, she could do just as well. At least that's what he hoped.

Over the wall the distance to the house looked a difficult course. There were o trees and at least 100-yards of slight incline to the back of the house. The ound was grass covered and plush with no places to hide.

"No cover at all," said Carla, slowly shaking her head as she examined the rd. Her jaw tightened and her lips pressed hard together in frustration. "I say e just B-line for the doors by the pool. No use trying to hide. He knows we're ere and I'm sure this place is set up with surveillance."

The big man nodded in total agreement and slid down the opposite side of the wall. Right on his heels Carla did the same. At a full sprint, the team of two ran up the grass hill then pressed their backs against the side of the house, waiting to see if there was any reaction from guards, dogs, or even The Butcher himself, but nothing–or no one–came. Just silence.

"I'll go in by the pool slider doors, but you go to the front of the house. Maybe we can squeeze this rat into a corner by coming at him from two sides."

Falau stared at his partner, unsure if splitting up was the right thing to do. Safety in numbers was always a rule that he lived by. Splitting off alone put them in a situation where they could end up in a one-on-one battle with an extremely dangerous man.

"Are you with me Falau?" snapped Carla.

"Yeah.

"Then stop staring at me and say something. We're kind of in a rush here. Are you good with the plan?"

Nodding his head in agreement the big man said, "Yeah. But if one of us gets in trouble, we yell. Just blow the cover to help each other."

"Done and done. Now go!"

Falau made his way up the embankment next to the house that allowed him a clear view of the driveway. The ground was laid in such a way to make the first floor of the house at ground level in front, and lower to make it ground level at the basement in the back.

Running to the corner he could see the back of the car The Butcher had been driving. The sharp pain of a flashback kicked inside his head.

"Not now!" he grunted to himself, keeping his feet moving and his mind on what needed to be done.

The car wasn't parked in any intentional way. It was half turned sideways and the garage door was open. The Butcher must've raced up the driveway and stopped the car as fast as he could and ran into the garage. But was he still in there?

Sliding out the .45 caliber handgun from the soft holster tucked into the back of his waistband, Falau held the gun deliberately in front of him and crept forward. He had a clear view of the far side of the garage, but Falau was blind to what lay closest to him, out of sight due to the corner. The garage was three-car wide and held a Mercedes, a Porsche, and now the crushed BMW.

Too many places to hide, he thought moving forward into the corner. *I could walk right into him.*

The big man rolled around the corner and dropped to one knee with the weapon straight out in front of him, revealing the closest section of the garage. Nothing.

He moved in and searched in and out of the cars but saw nothing that provided a clue to where The Butcher was. Only one thing was sure, and that was that he was not hiding in the garage.

On the back wall three steps led up to a door that had been left ajar. Sliding to get a glimpse of what lay inside, but still keeping a safe distance, all that could be seen was a tile floor that ran up to the threshold. It was a hallway. *People tend not to tile the inside of closets,* thought Falau.

Climbing the steps to the door he looked deeper inside and found only darkness. The Butcher was drawing him further into the house. He knew the layout of the house. He knew where the furniture was. He knew the places to hide. In the dark, they would be vigilantes who would have to move at a snail's pace to not bump into anything and give the killer a reference point to shoot at.

Slipping through the door a 20-foot hallway stretched in front of him, and opened into a large kitchen. Try as he might to be silent, Falau still created ample sound in the silence of the house as his shoes echoed off the tile floor. There was door on the opposite wall of the counters. It was glass. Inside the door the steps were covered in carpet, and led down to the basement.

Moving to the far end of the kitchen he found a set of French doors already open, and which led to a sunken living room and a plush carpet to muffle the sound of his footsteps.

The living room was wide open. A sectional sofa lined the back and side wall. There was nowhere to hide in this room. It was designed for entertainment, but could also give a clear shot to anyone moving across it. Keeping to the wall was the safest bet. Walls will cover your back as long as you keep your eyes sharp. Moving in front of the TV, that was laid into the wall with a custom-built entertainment center, the big man could see that the stairs came down as he got to the other side of the room. The steps were covered in carpet, but the chance of them creaking was difficult to assess. Getting caught in the middle of a set of steps was the worst of all situations; nowhere to run or hide. Trapped, with just up or down to choose from while bullets flew your way from those same two directions? No good! There was really no choice. Upstairs had to be searched, and now was the time.

Up two, three, five, eight steps, with all the sound of a church mouse. Yet Falau still feared the creak or moan from the steps would give away his position.

Creak!

From down the steps and around the corner the sound of an un-oiled hinge landed firmly in the ear Falau. "The basement door," he whispered to himself.

But was it Carla coming up, or The Butcher going down? The risk was too big to wait and find out. The big man moved down the steps with purpose, though as stealthy as he could in the situation. Running into a trap filled with gunfire was not what he wanted to do. His feet slid across the living room rug and he stopped at the corner.

If tactics had taught him anything, it would be that The Butcher would be waiting with his gun sited on him as he turned the corner. Taking a deep breath and pressing his back against the wall, he revealed himself as he burst around the corner and dropped to one knee.

"Freeze!" screamed Carla from one floor below.

As the words registered with Falau he heard two shots ring out from the basement. Without hesitation, he ran to the basement door in the kitchen and swung it open. Flying down the steps he could hear the backslider of the basement slam shut and the sound of heavy feet crossing the cement that surrounded the pool and fading into the distance.

The basement was another location for entertainment, with a bar and a pool table, but next to the pool table laid a body, motionless and unmistakabl the shape of a woman.

With his heart rate quickening with fear and his vision blurring with tears Falau moved as fast as he could to Carla. No longer worried about getting sho at or completing the mission, he had only one thing on his mind, and that wa saving his new partner.

Sliding to his knees and stopping right next to her he could see her gaspin for air as blood streamed from her mouth.

He soon spotted a red spot on her shirt, increasing in size as the second wore on. It was on the left side of her chest close to her heart.

"You're okay!" said Falau out of instinct, and he placed his hand over he wound trying desperately to stop the bleeding.

"I will get you out of here! You're fine!"

"No... I am... not," said Carla with a faint smile and looking into the eyes of the big man. She placed her hand onto his, the one trying to stop the bleeding. Grabbing it tight she moved it away from the wound and squeezed it. "Make this worth it."

"What?" Falau asked, leaning closer.

"Make this worth it. For my brothers."

Blankness settled on his face as he looked down at his dying friend. She knew her fate and she wasn't fighting. She coughed hard as the blood filled her lungs and shot from her mouth. Falau held her body tight in his arms as she trembled until she trembled no more.

Chapter 18

As Carla's head was laid to rest on the carpet of the basement floor, the sound of the creaking door and footsteps coming down the steps signaled Falau The Butcher was coming.

Falau picked up Carla's Ruger SR9C 9mm handgun and tucked it into his waistband for safe keeping.

Ducking behind the pool table, he held his pistol tight.

Bang!

A shot cut through the air, ricocheting off the slate top of the pool tabl and embedding in the wall.

"Who are you? What do you want with me?" questioned The Butcher wit more hate in his voice than confusion. "You know how many cops I've killed You think I'm afraid to kill a cop? If you run now you may have a chance to ge away. I am not as fast as I once was."

"I was sent to offer you a deal."

"The kind of deal where you attack me? I'm not a fool. You are here to ki me."

The sound of footsteps retreating back up the steps and was clear as day. Th Butcher wanted a game of cat and mouse. He could work the room, drawin his prey into the open.

If he had a cell phone with him, Falau was sure that guards would alread be on their way. The time to make a move was now, or the moment would sli away forever.

Arriving at the steps he used his gun to sweep across, making sure they wer clear. The door had been left open at the top of the steps. Falau stopped shy c running through it and held back. He knew better, and took his time again. H started at one side of the room and worked his way across, looking through the site of his pistol.

Bang!

A shot splintered the door frame on the far side where Falau stood. Checking the angle of the impact into the doorframe, he worked out the shot had come from the living room. Falau finally turned the gun around the corner, firing two shots to provide himself with cover. After firing the shots he slid across the floor behind the kitchen island. His location was blown by the simple sound of his shoes hitting the tile floor, but the island provided more secure cover.

"You should not have killed her. That was a big mistake! It changes everything," said Falau, trying to draw a response from the killer so he'd give up his position.

"Why? Did you love her?"

Pausing and quickly putting together his thoughts, he knew the answer was not that clear-cut. It was not love or hate, or anything so juvenile. It was deeper, despite the limited time he knew her.

"No. Much worse than love. I respected her," Falau called back, feeling a lump in his throat. It had been so long since he had respected anyone, including himself. His life has been filled with a series of rejects and losers for the last five years. Carla had changed that. She had purpose, honor, and passion for what was right, even if she had to do the wrong thing to make it right. "You're going to pay for what you have done."

Reaching down he removed his shoes, placing them on the floor behind the island. Inching forward to the front of the island, his eyes started to adjust to the darkness, his footsteps now silent with nothing but a sock touching the floor.

The Butcher was not on the right side of the living room. "Too bad you are not smart enough to run. But it is survival of the fittest. The stupid must die for us all to get stronger," called the voice now coming from the far side of the living room.

Quickly moving to the edge of the double doorway Falau again started to cut the room with his gun. Slow and methodical, checking every inch. No mistake could be afforded now he was this close. Despite The Butcher's words he knew that this night would end up with one of them dead. He would fail in his mission, but maybe he could avenge Carla's death.

He stepped down to the living room, training his gun at the banister that ran down the wall next to him, ending at the far end of the room. If the chance of a shot came, he would take it. Shoot him dead. One shot, two shots, three shots... it didn't matter. Just end the sorry son of a bitch's life and be done with it.

"Never thought a guy called The Butcher would run and hide. Such a coward," called out Falau, waiting for a response. But The Butcher was not saying a word, keeping his location hidden.

Getting down low, Falau crept close to the wall below where the banister came down. The killer's voice was not coming from above... his last words were from the adjoining room, waiting for the big man to show himself and walk straight into the line of fire, Falau was sure that The Butcher was waiting for him.

Suddenly, from over the banister flew a man with a great scar running down his cheek, and The Butcher crashed down, knocking Falau to the ground and causing Falau's gun to fly from his hands.

The Butcher quickly wrapped a cord around Falau's neck, and tightened it as hard as he could. Falau forced his fingers into the loop, slipping them under the cord and trying to keep the blood flowing to his head.

"You're going to learn why they call me El Carnicero! No easy death, no like with the girl. I am going to put you on display for everyone to see."

His face pressed hard into the side of Falau's face, as spit shot from hi mouth and sweat dripped from his face.

The feeling of panic started to overwhelm Falau from a lack of oxygen. He'd felt this way once before when he was a young boy. He went swimming in th ocean and was pulled under by the waves, looking for air when there wasn't an there.

He tried to throw his elbows back at his attacker and kick him, but it ha little effect. The man was too strong and the cord was doing its job.

The cord started to cut into his neck. His fingers were doing nothing t prevent cutting off the circulation. The big man's eyes started to roll in his hea and his world began to turn gray.

"I'm not going to kill you now. I am going to keep you alive and just kill you a little bit each day in my basement. Let you look at that whore of a friend. This is what happens to people who want to confront The Butcher. You will be lucky to have died by my hands."

The sound of a gun cocking stopped the words spilling from The Butcher's mouth. His grip loosened. Falau pulled the cord away from his neck and dropped to the ground on his hands and knees, gasping for air. Color flooded back into his vision and his head felt clearer again.

"Get up and stand against the wall with that piece of trash," commanded the voice.

"Who the hell are you?" asked The Butcher, pointing his finger at the man.

"My name is Carlos Rivera, with the National Police Special Operations Commandos. Now shut up the hell up."

Falau pulled himself up and looked at the man from the National Police. He was young and brash. Falau immediately liked him.

"You're a cop?" he asked.

"National Police."

"Sorry. I'm kind of in the same line of work that you are, but more of a ounty hunter. I have some people that want to see this guy on trial for all the rug running."

"That's fine, but you two are going to jail until I find out who killed the girl. omebody's going to pay for that."

"Let me take the sick freak out of here, and I can make sure he pays."

"Shut up!" demanded Rivera. "You really think I will let the two of you walk ut of here?"

"I have $1million in cash and will give it to you now if you let me leave. Do ith him what you will," interjected The Butcher.

Shaking his head Falau again turned his attention back to the National Po-ce man.

"Can I shut this guy up for us?"

"Sure."

Removing the small injection kit from his shirt collar–just where Tyler said would be–he jabbed it into the neck of The Butcher, causing the killer to lash ut at him. Rubbing his neck, the killer pulled the needle from his neck and he ll to the floor.

"That's better," said Falau.

"Why do they want him? The people you work for?"

"He has killed a lot of people with the drugs he's smuggled. He cuts it with Carfentanil. They want to give him another trial which is not so public."

"You know I can't just let him just walk away."

"I understand," replied Falau, rubbing his chin with his thumb and finger. "But what if I could give you something more valuable than this jerk. What if I can hand you the biggest drug bust in the history of Colombia?"

The National Policeman stood still and trained his gun on Falau. He was weighing his options and deciding if he could trust him.

"It's a simple choice. You could shoot me or you could be a huge hero. It's up to you."

Carlos Rivera lowered his gun and smiled. "Tell me what you know."

Chapter 19

ulling down to the loading bay, the hearse backed up, bumping its backdoor gainst the rear entrance to McGinty's Funeral Parlor. The engine shut down nd the driver slid the door open.

Stepping from the hearse Falau looked up to the sky, seeking few stars. "Mi-mi, you kill the stars with the streetlights."

Walking up to the door he knocked in the specific pattern he had been in-ructed to by Tyler. Knocking out the signal let the men inside know it was im. Slowly the metal door slid open, revealing two large men who stepped for-ard and opened the back of the hearse without saying a word.

"Hey old friend," chirped Tyler inside the doorway. "Congratulations on our first successful mission."

"Thanks," Falau responded in a somber tone. "There was a heavy price to ay."

"I heard. She was one of the best. My guess is he hit her with a lucky shot."

"Not lucky for her."

"No."

Tyler held his hand out, making sure Falau knew he was happy with the ork he had done.

"You did an amazing job. Carla knew the risks but wanted to be part of is one. She would be proud of you. You made him pay for her death and the eaths of a lot of other people."

Falau looked to the floor and grunted in passive agreement. He was not re how he felt about the whole thing. People were now dead and nothing ould bring them back.

"Come inside."

"I'm just going to head back home."

"No! Come on man, just come in for a few minutes and have some coffee."

Tyler wrapped his arm around his friend and led them into a hallway now half covered by the coffin that had been in the back of the hearse.

"Is he in there?" asked Tyler.

"Yeah. He started to stink."

"I know. It's disgusting. But that's what happens."

Tyler placed his hands on the coffin, pushing it off its perch on the rollers. The wooden box hit the floor, smashing on the concrete before the body of The Butcher tumbled onto the floor.

The killer's eyes locked on the men around him as he struggled to get free of the bonds that tied his hands and feet. His mouth was covered in duct tape.

"Men, take out the trash to the main room. It's time for trial."

"Trial? Now?"

"Yeah, the judges are here. This will all be over in just a few minutes. By the way, everyone is very impressed you used one of his smuggling coffins to ship him back."

"I thought it was a nice touch," said Falau with a smile as they walked to the open door at the end of the hallway.

Chapter 20

The room would normally hold wakes, but had been cleared of the normal chairs and tables. Under where the casket normally sat there was a single chair The Butcher was positioned in. A single muted light bulb shone down upon him. A crucifix hung on the wall behind him, looking down on him during this time of his judgment. To his right along the wall sat nine empty high-backed chairs, but none of the people in the room made a move to occupy them. Clearly they were for the judges.

On the opposite side of the room were a few people in attendance. Falau, Tyler, four other men and two women, who made no attempt to interact with anyone at any time. The operation was all business... there was no time for anything but the task at hand.

One of the larger men walked over and ripped the tape from The Butcher's mouth, taking part of his facial hair with it.

"Fuck you!" screeched The Butcher, spitting on the man who ripped the tape from his mouth. "Let me go, I swear I will kill you all. What the hell is this, playtime for you people? Get me the fuck out here!"

"Silence. You will have your chance to speak," responded the man now covered in spit.

"Let me go!"

In one smooth motion, the man spun back to The Butcher and jammed a revolver into his mouth. "I asked you to be silent, and told you you would have chance to speak. Do you understand me this time?"

The Butcher nodded as his eyes focused on the man's finger lightly dusting over the trigger.

"Good. Thank you."

Removing the gun from his mouth the man walked away as The Butcher took a deep breath and examined the room. Making eye contact with Falau at the far end, he stared hard.

Falau lifted his glass, as if he was toasting the man. "I don't think he likes me."

"Think you're right. But he seems like he could be a hard guy to get along with," Tyler responded with a smirk.

On the far side of the room a door slid open, and silence fell across the room. All eyes moved to the door, waiting with anticipation. Falau did as all the others did, but had no idea why. The feeling that something would be missed if he looked away was overwhelming.

One by one nine people entered the room. They ranged in height and weight, but they all had one thing in common: you could not see any part of their bodies. All the judge's robes covered them from their neck to their feet, including their arms. It was impossible to see their hands. A hood even covered their hair, while black and white masks covered their faces. Falau thought they looked like the comedy and tragedy masks you'd see at the theater. The differ- ence was, these masks all had different expressions on them, everything from horror to happiness. It was impossible to detect any real emotion from any o the judges wearing the uniform they had devised.

The judges found their seats and sat down, and still they didn't speak. They looked straight ahead and interacted with nobody in the room. Falau knew without being told that the judges were off limits. There was to be no friendl chitchat. No asking how the family was, or if they're enjoying their stay. Thei anonymity was paramount and, nobody was going to get in the way of that.

"Step back against the wall," requested Tyler. "We can't interfere in any wa or he goes free. The rules are very strict to make sure everything works out fo the best."

Leaning back against the wall, Falau thought if they let the sick piece c garbage go after all he went through to get him, and especially after Carla diec he would lose his mind.

A man in his late 50s stepped to the center of the room. He wore a wel fitting suit that looked to be in the $300 range. Nice, but off the rack and nc custom-made. Life had taken its toll on the man. He bore deep wrinkles an thinned hair that was approaching fully gray. He stood with a slight hunc and needed reading glasses, the kind that many old folks wore in the movies that sat at the end of their noses. Despite running over the various situations in his head, Falau could come up with no reason that would explain how this man ended up working with this kind of group. How was he involved with the judges and bringing people to justice?

The man cleared his throat and raised his hand, showing that he wanted silence in an already silent room.

"Good evening. You have decided to bear witness to the trial of Roberto Mallarino, otherwise known as The Butcher." The man moved his hand, indicating the man tied up against the wall.

"What kind of shit is this? I had a trial and was found innocent," squawked the stone-cold killer.

"Sir, I informed you that you will have a chance to speak. I do not want to have to muzzle you for the rest of these proceedings."

The Butcher snorted with contempt, but resisted speaking out again. Falau was impressed this man could shut him up with words, and not the insertion of a pistol into his mouth as the other man had used.

"Sir, you are hereby charged with drug trafficking, murder, murder by drug trafficking, criminal conspiracy, corruption of government officials, and you are fully responsible for the deaths of 384 Floridians in the last two years, due to drugs you bring into the area cut with Carfentanil, and countless deaths in Columbia. How do you plead?"

The Butcher squinted his eyes and tilted his head to the side. "How do I plead? You want to know how I plead? I was tried by my home country of Colombia and found innocent. This isn't even a courtroom! You have me in a funeral home for the trial, so you can just kill me and dump me in a grave! Well, screw you all!"

"Sir, do you plead innocent or guilty? If you do not provide a plea, we'll take your silence as a plea of guilt."

The man in the suit stared at The Butcher. "Your answer, Sir? Now."

"You people are insane! I'm innocent! Innocent of everything they say I have done!" snapped The Butcher, struggling to break the binds that held his hands.

"The plea is innocence. The questions will now start." The man in the suit walked over to the judges and made his way to one that sat last in line. A gloved hand slid out from under the robe holding a stack of index cards, and handed them to the man, pointing to the top one. Without any conversation, the man in the suit moved back to the center of the room and faced The Butcher.

Falau watched the interaction intently and realize in the judges spoke to nobody. Nothing about their identity was going to be known to anybody even the sound of their words. He wondered if Tyler was the only one who had any real contact with the judges.

"Sir. Have you ever trafficked drugs to the United States?"

"Ever?"

"Sir, please answer the questions as they are asked. Have you ever trafficked drugs to the United States?"

"Yes. I was a young man. Just one time. My family needed the money for—"

"A simple yes or no will do," interrupted the man in the suit.

"Did you traffic drugs into Miami?"

"Yes, the one time—"

"That's good," interrupted the man in the suit again.

"Did you ever cut your drugs with Carfentanil?"

The Butcher looked over to the judges and then scanned the room. His face hardened as he nodded. "You all think you're so much better than me but I do what I have to to survive. I pulled myself up from nothing and look what I have achieved. Now you think you can pass judgment on me?"

"That's exactly what these judges are here to do," snapped the man flipping to the next card. "Did you sell your drugs to Juan Martinez in Miami?"

"Yes! So what? What does it matter if I did? It was his choice who he sold the drugs too. He was the one killing people by pushing it on the streets."

"Martinez is dead. He tested his shipment. Not even a large amount, but it killed him."

Watching The Butcher's face go blank Falau could see for the first time he had been shaken.

The Judge who had given the index cards raised his hand into a 'stop' position. The man in the suit walked back to the judge and handed the index cards to him. He also handed a small piece of paper to each judge and returned to the center of the room.

"The judges will now deliberate, and we will have a verdict momentarily."

"Wait a minute! He said I would have a chance to speak. I want to say some things!"

"You did have a chance to speak. You had your say when you answered the question. That's all they needed to hear from you."

A tapping sound emanated from the head judge as his foot repeatedly hit the floor, stopping the conversation. The man walked back over and collected the paper from the judges. Placing himself back at the center of the room, he held the card in front of him looked down his nose through his glasses to read the fate of The Butcher.

"The judges have come to a unanimous verdict."

On those words, the judges stood up in unison and marched single file out the same door they entered through. Falau was sure they would be gone from the premises well before any action was taken.

"On all accounts, you have been found guilty as charged. Sentence will only be carried out on the charge of the deaths of 384 people as a result of drug trafficking, and of cutting the drugs with a known lethal substance."

"You can't do this! You have no right to find me guilty of anything! I want a lawyer!"

"You are hereby sentenced to death within the next hour, and may God have mercy on your soul."

"What? No! You can't—" The Butcher was silenced by a strip of duct tape over his mouth. Struggling back and forth, he fell to the floor in a panic and several men converged on him and removed him from the room.

"Ladies and gentlemen," said the man in the suit. "Justice has been served. Let's go now and forget anything ever happened here. Take care."

The man with the simple suit and years of work etched into his face tucked his glasses into the front pocket of his jacket and walked out the door.

Chapter 21

The door of the coffee shop two buildings down from Falau's apartment swung open with a hard push from Falau.

Entering the shop he ran his eyes over the room and saw Tyler sitting at the furthest booth. Tyler always placed himself in a position of power by facing the door and having his back to the wall. Nobody could sneak up on him from that position. Was it intentional, or was it just habit at this point for his friend to be on high alert?

Scanning his eyes over everyone in the room, Falau felt his senses were onc again alive. He was running on instinct, and the sharpness of his mind was fan tastic. The room was safe and he knew it. He knew the people who were th greatest risk, and he knew those who were not. He knew who had a gun an who didn't. He was back on track in every sense of the word, despite the diffi culties of he'd witnessed.

"How are things going?" said the big man, sliding into a seat opposite hi old friend.

"Things are always great when the world becomes a safer place overnight smirked Tyler as he raised a cup of coffee, using it point at the TV set hig above the counter.

The national news was showing a smiling man standing in front of a mou tain of cocaine. He held up two automatic weapons and was awash in the flash es of camera bulbs exploding in his face. Across the bottom of the screen banner with yellow letters surrounded by red, read: 'Lt. Carlos Rivera of th National Police of Colombia makes the biggest drug arrest in the history o South America.' A handsome man came back to the TV broadcasting live fro Colombia. "More than 2000 kilos of cocaine and over 100 kilos of heroin we confiscated in the early morning hours at the Jet International import and e port facility in Bogotá, Colombia. The result of this massive confiscation could limit the sales of drugs all over the United States and Europe."

"That's one happy cop," said Tyler with a smile. He took a sip off his coffee and placed it on the table.

"National Police. I hear they are touchy about that kind of thing..." said Falau.

"That should put him on the fast track to the top command. He could be a good man to know if you're ever in that part of the world. Who knows what he could help a guy with in the future?"

Tyler was right. Rivera was now a major contact and someone who was willing to work with him if the price was right and if Falau could provide him with another big bust. If the judges were big on getting smugglers in Colombia, this was going to be an outstanding contact.

"Yeah he would be."

Tyler shifted in his seat and reached for his briefcase. Flipping the locks to open it, he removed a plain brown oversized envelope, the kind that most offices use for interoffice mail. He placed the envelope on the table and slid it across to Falau.

The envelope was thick, and sealed closed with red twine that linked around two red circles attached with string.

"This is for you."

Picking up the envelope , Falau opened the top and could see inside several small packs of money. All US currency, in denominations of $10, $20, and $100 bills that all looked used and dirty. There was no way they were counterfeit or had markings of any kind of sequential order. Nothing about the money would link him to the judges in any way. They were perfectly random.

"Thanks," said Falau, wrapping the red string around the circles again. "Feels good to be on the side of the good guys. I was starting to wonder if I was still one of the good guys now."

"Falau, there was never any doubt in my mind that you were still one of the good guys."

A large heavy-set waitress wearing a nametag reading Helen stood at the end of the table. "You want something to eat?" she grunted at Falau.

"Tell me something..." Tyler glanced up to read the nametag. "...Helen. Looking at this guy right now, would you say he is one of the good guys?"

"My name ain't Helen. It's Ruth. I forgot my name-tag today. He's a good guy if he leaves a good tip. Want coffee or food?"

"Coffee is fine," said Falau with another smile.

"Great, I'm sure there will be a good tip on a $.99 cup of coffee," moaned Ruth as she walked away from the table.

"See, even Ruth knows you're one of the good guys, and you always have been. You've just had some tough times."

"Wish I could believe that. Maybe in time I can see things right."

"You can do it with us. If this is the work for you I've been told it's okay to give you more assignments. You wouldn't exactly be part of the inner circle, but you would play a vital role in the success of the operation."

Falau looked down at the table and placed his hands behind his neck. He rubbed hard, as if he was trying to ease away a muscle knot.

"I don't know. I almost got myself killed down there. If not for some luck I would've failed."

"But you didn't. You succeeded. For whatever reason, you came out on top That's all that matters. You're getting your chops back. You're like a great jazz musician. You just can't pick up from where you left off after not playing for years and try to sit down with Miles Davis and knock out a few tunes. It takes time. I know you don't like to talk about your past but you need to accept it. It's who you are."

"I don't know what to tell you."

"Tell me you'll think about it. No need to decide here and now. Just call me if you could use some work, even if it's only part-time." Tyler reach into the pocket of the suit jacket and pulled out a card very similar to the one he gave Falau before. The only writing on it was the phone number.

"Take care of yourself, my friend. Was great seeing you again," said Tyler as he stood up and placed his hand on Falau's shoulder, squeezing it while looking down into his eyes. "Just don't wait too long if you want to be on the job. My bosses tend to like consistency, and to know what's going on all the time. I will hold the spot as long as I can. The fixer can't take forever."

"Is that what the judges call me? The fixer." Falau said with a wide smile.

"No. I am the fixer. I fix problems and I can't take forever to get back to them." Explained Tyler with a slight laugh. "Take care."

Tyler patted Falau's shoulder one last time and walked towards the door. Falau looked at the card in his hand and spun it between his fingers. Even with all the risk and Carla's death, Falau was feeling better now than he had in years. The flashbacks had been gone for almost a week and his drinking had slowed. He felt like he had something to live for, and that was a feeling that had left him a long time ago.

"Where did your buddy go?" Ruth said, placing the coffee in front of Falau with a small splash. "Hun. He didn't even leave you with a few bucks to cover the cost of his coffee. Some friend he is."

Ruth rumbled away, her words echoing in Falau's ears. "Some friend he is." And she was right. He is some friend. The kind of friend that looks after you when you're at the worst point in your life. One who comes in and bales your ass out when you're getting ready to end it all.

That kind of friend is a best friend.

Pulling the cell phone from his pocket the big man quickly dialed the num-er on the card, stopping Tyler right outside the coffee shop.

"Ya... Tyler."

"Falau. Stay there."

Falau shoved some money on the table and jumped up, moving to the door s fast as he could. Pushing the door open, he tried not to run to Tyler and ause too many eyes to look at his old friend. Falau detected at least two cars in he area he was sure Tyler would soon be followed by. Quickening his pace, he eached Tyler and caught his breath.

"One more assignment, just to see how things go."

Extending his arm, Tyler smiled as Falau shook hands with him. "Falau, I eel really good about this."

Suddenly they heard screaming from inside the coffee shop. Falau and Tyler urned to look, and saw Ruth crying and holding the hundred dollar bill Falau ad left for her.

Falau shrugged his shoulders. "She earned it with her sunny disposition."

Additional Information

Did you enjoy what you just read? If so please take a few minutes to write a review. It helps out more than you know. Reviews help independent authors get their books shown to more people and that helps us sell more book. With that money, we turn around and write more books for you to enjoy! Thank you for any help and taking the time to review THE FIXER.

IF YOU WANT TO FIND more books by Mike Gomes and some free offers please go to the website at mikegomeswrites.com and join the mailing list.

30996359R00058

Made in the USA
Lexington, KY
14 February 2019